The words sliced Rosa's heart into two. She looked away. *How could I know, Johnny, that Trent was just using me to rebel against his family?*

"You said he lives far away," Marc said. With this, he swung Johnny up to ride on his shoulders.

This special treat, however, didn't distract her son.

"Yeah, but he's visited me before," Johnny said. "I remember him."

"Johnny, people are the way they are." Marc let Johnny down. Then he stooped to look him in the eye. "Only God can change a heart and only when the person wants their heart to change."

"You think my daddy's heart needs changing?" Johnny asked. "Is it a bad heart?"

"Not bad, Johnny. He just needs to understand more about loving others. That's all I meant," Marc said. "If you were my son, I wouldn't let you out of my life. I wouldn't want to live far away from you."

Rosa experienced the truth of these words. They coiled around her heart.

Johnny wrapped his arms around Marc's neck. "I want to be your son. Couldn't you marry us?"

Books by Lyn Cote

LYN COTE

Lyn Cote and her husband, her real-life hero, became in-laws recently when their son married his true love. Lyn already loves her daughter-in-law and enjoys this new adventure in family stretching. Lyn and her husband still live on the lake in the north woods, where they watch a bald eagle and its young soar and swoop overhead throughout the year. She wishes the best to all her readers. You may e-mail Lyn at l.cote@juno.com or write her at P.O. Box 864, Woodruff, WI 54548. And drop by her blog www.strongwomenbravestories.blogspot.com to read stories of strong women in real life and in true-to-life fiction. "Every woman has a story. Share yours."

Shelter of Hope
Lyn Cote

Steeple
Hill®

Published by Steeple Hill Books™

STEEPLE HILL BOOKS

Steeple
Hill®

Recycling programs
for this product may
not exist in your area.

ISBN-13: 978-0-373-87621-1

SHELTER OF HOPE

www.SteepleHill.com

Printed in U.S.A.

Come to me, all you who are weary and burdened, and I will give you rest. Take my yoke upon you and learn from me, for I am gentle and humble in heart, and you will find rest for your souls. For my yoke is easy and my burden is light.

—*Matthew* 11:28–30

To DeeDee, a great knitter and a better friend

Chapter One

Without warning, on a clear blue August morning, danger barreled onto New Friends Street. Glancing over his shoulder, Marc Chambers saw the cement truck take the corner a little fast. At the same moment, he glimpsed a boy running across the street. Not looking. *No!*

The cement truck's brakes squealed like a trapped animal. Marc raced for the kid. Scooped him up. The wheels of the cement truck, just feet away, jumped, skipped—trying to stop in time.

People were screaming. Marc wrapped himself around the small boy's body. Threw himself into a roll…

I can't stop in time. The horrible wrenching sound of metal chewing into metal churned through his flesh like the grinding of some vicious machine. His heart pounded in his ears—

"Marc," a familiar voice came through the din in Marc's head. "Marc, it's all right. You and the boy are safe. The truck missed you both."

Marc blinked. His mind tried to grasp his grandmother's words. What had just happened to him?

Marc looked into his grandmother's soft round face, surrounded by her wavy white hair and straw hat. Her kind bluc eyes were dark with concern. He realized suddenly that other people were crowded around him. Staring at him.

Then he heard—felt—the boy in his arms sobbing. He released him. Marc shook his head as if that could shake off what had just happened or what had just flashed through his mind.

A pretty young woman claimed the boy and encircled him with her arms. "You could have been killed, Johnny!" she cried out. "You could have been killed!" She sank to her knees, clutching the boy to her.

Marc slowly pulled himself up until he was sitting with his back against the curb. He held his head in his hands, not trusting himself to speak or to try to rise. His stomach sloshed back and forth in a giddy tide. A deluge of memories wanted to saturate him with fear and carry him back to January, back to that awful day.

"*Man,*" someone with a deep, gruff voice said loudly. "Man, am I glad you were able to get to him. I couldn't have stopped in time."

Marc glanced toward the voice.

It came from a man in gray work clothes. He was sort of leaning limply over the back fender of the cement truck. "I don't know what I would have done. I got kids of my own."

I don't know what I would have done. The man's words sent shivers through Marc. And from the corner of his eye, he saw the same shivers go through the young denim-clad woman. Life was so fragile—he'd learned that lesson this year painfully. He put out a hand and patted the woman's slender shoulder awkwardly, briefly.

A horn honked and then another. Marc looked around at the crowd in the middle of the street and the cars that had halted on either side of them.

A new brisk voice, a woman's voice, intruded. "Let's all get out of the street. We're blocking traffic."

The people around Marc moved away reluctantly, returning to the dedication at the Habitat site. Many kept casting glances back at him. Marc tried to avoid their gazes, and calm the roiling in his midsection. The truck driver climbed into his rig and drove off much slower.

Marc's grandmother lingered protectively beside him. That bothered him. He didn't want her worrying again. He forced a smile and glanced up. "Go on. I'll be all right. It's just the heat and running like that. The excitement—that's all." *I thought I'd put it behind me. What just happened?*

Another older woman with salt-and-pepper hair was standing by the young mother who was still on her knees. "Rosa," she began, "*por favor...*"

He couldn't follow what she said after that; it sounded like Spanish, sounded worried.

"No, *Abuela,* Grandmother," the young woman said, shaking her head. "You go. I'll come...soon."

His own grandmother tucked her hand into the Spanish-speaking grandmother's elbow. "Come. We'll go and let them have a few moments to compose themselves."

"*Si,*" the woman agreed in a pleasantly accented voice, "yes, I must represent *la familia.*" Still, the woman looked concerned.

The two grandmothers walked together across New Friends Street to watch the dedication of the Habitat for Humanity house that was being built in their little town of Hope, Wisconsin. August heat, dripping with humidity, wrapped around Marc. It made it harder to breathe, harder to calm his racing heart.

The mother of the boy looked at him and then slid from her knees to sit beside him against the curb. The little boy sank between them, leaning against her. "I'm Rosa Santos." She offered him her hand. "And this is Johnny."

She still looked shaken. He forced another smile, a reassuring one. He gripped her small hand in his for a brief moment, comforted by touching her soft palm. "Marc Chambers."

"Thank you so much," Rosa said, feathering the boy's bangs with one hand. "Thank you for saving my Johnny." Her voice caught on the boy's name.

He looked into the woman's pretty face, her olive skin smooth and lightly tanned. Her large eyes—so brown they were almost black—captured him. Not only because they were beautiful, but because fear blazed there.

He had experienced that kind of flaming, consuming fear. Evidently it still lived in him. *I thought I got over all this.* He sucked in the hot, moist air. "No problem." He shuddered involuntarily. "No problem."

Then he noticed the boy, Johnny, was looking down, looking shamed. It cut into Marc's heart.

Marc bent his head to eye level with the boy. "Johnny, that's your name, right?" Marc waited till the boy had nodded, bouncing his brown bangs. Then with his hand, he lifted Johnny's trembling chin and looked into the boy's tear-streaked face. "It's okay. We weren't hurt. Just be more careful next time. Look before you cross." *Even when a man doesn't take foolish chances, bad can happen.*

Rosa's heart still pounded against her ribs like a wild bird trying to escape from a cage. How could she have let this happen? Johnny had been standing right beside her. Then she'd heard the truck's brakes squealing and seen her son running into the truck's path. She had to get her emotions under control. She didn't want to raise a fearful child, just a careful one.

Rosa's heartbeat began to slow as she stared at the picture of this man, Marc Chambers, comforting her boy. He was a big man. His legs stretched out long and strong. His hand was tanned brown by the sun and his hair was light brown with a reddish tone, his expression filled with compassion.

"I saw a dog running across the street," her son mumbled. "I wanted to…" Johnny tried to lower his chin again.

A dog. All this because of a stray dog. Rosa closed her eyes for a moment. The image of Johnny running into the path of the oncoming truck was now burned into her memory. She opened her eyes, hoping the glittering sunshine would blot it out.

Then Marc softened his voice and let his hand fall back to his side. "Just be more careful next time, okay? Bad things can happen in this world."

Johnny nodded while she repeated what this kind man had said. Bad things could happen in this world, *had* happened to her. She looked away so neither of them would see her blinking away a tear.

"Should we join the others?" Marc asked.

She turned and looked fully into his blue eyes. She read concern there and something else lurked in their recesses. "A little while longer, please." Her knees still felt like soft-set gelatin.

He nodded and glanced across the street.

She appreciated his not questioning her or urging her to do what she couldn't yet. "It's just because…" Her voice faltered. She looked down at the pebbles along the curb. Should she say this with her son listening?

Marc made a sound, something like a chuckle. "My mom always points to the gray hairs my brother and I gave her. She claims she can name each gray hair by incident."

His unexpected understanding nearly undid her

composure. Then his humorous comment about his mother knowing which incident caused each of her gray hairs made her smile. It was just what she needed to help her come back to herself. "I'm ready now." She started to get up.

"Let me help you." Rising, Marc offered her both his hands. She took them and he pulled her to her feet. His strength flowed through her hands and up her arms. Marc released her hands and she immediately missed their reassuring support.

She noticed then that he had grazed the side of his face which had been away from her. She claimed his chin and turned his face, examining it. Then she blushed at doing something so personal to a man she'd just met. "Sorry, but I'm so used to bumps and scratches. Here."

Avoiding his gaze, she dug into her jean pocket, pulling out a plastic pack. She waved it. "I came prepared." She lifted out a square packet antiseptic swab, tore it open and wiped the grazed flesh. And did the same to his lower arm, hand and wrist which also had been scraped. The sensation of touching him was peculiar, made her a little breathless. "There, that will help start the healing." She made her voice strong, masking how being this close to him affected her.

"Thanks." He looked uncomfortable and pained.

"I have ibuprofen—"

"No, I'm fine," he said, holding up the uninjured hand. "Just bumped and scraped a bit. I'll live."

She wanted to pursue this but recognized his dismissal. She looked down at Johnny. "Before you lead me across the street, look both ways first, please," she said, stopping her son from running across the street again.

"*Si, Mama.*" Johnny looked both ways. "We can go now."

She ruffled her son's hair and reached for Marc's hand

again. She didn't speak a word but tried to convey to him with a smile her gratitude once more.

He squeezed her hand, dropped it and reached for Johnny's hand. So did she.

The three of them walked across the street, linked together. Somehow this lifted her mood. At the curb, they parted and joined the crowd listening to the end of the dedication. Marc murmured a few polite words and drifted away. She took a deep breath, trying to appear normal. Her emotions, however, did not obey her will.

Rosa had met the woman speaking, Eleanor Washburn, who would be coordinating the project. Trying to listen to Eleanor, Rosa folded her arms in front of her and covered her mouth with her hand. She didn't want anybody to see her lips still trembling. She captured her lower lip with her upper teeth, willing them to still.

Eleanor said, "Without arguing over theological differences, *everyone* can put love into action by swinging a hammer as an instrument to demonstrate God's love."

Rosa couldn't stop herself from glancing toward the man who'd saved her son. There was so much she'd wanted to say. How could she let him know how grateful she was? Words didn't seem enough. And somehow his expression had warned her away.

At the front, Eleanor beamed at everyone. "To date, Habitat volunteers and supporters have made decent, affordable housing a reality for more than three hundred thousand families worldwide. Now I'd like you all to meet the Santos family." During the applause, she waved at Rosa to come forward.

Rosa swallowed down the tears that were still trying to surface. She took her grandmother and Johnny's hands and led them forward. Eleanor smiled and turned them to face the crowd. "Rosa, why don't you introduce yourself and your family?"

Rosa swallowed again. Her throat was thick. "I'm Rosa Santos." Her voice cracked on her last name. "This is my grandmother, Consuela Santos, and my son, Johnny." An embarrassing tear trickled down her cheek. She tried to ignore it. "We are very happy to have this opportunity for a new home of our own." More tears slid down her cheeks. She tried to rein them in and failed. "Thank you all for coming to help us."

Ignoring Eleanor's prompting for her to say more, Rosa hurried her small but very precious family back to where they had been standing. That of course was the problem. Her family had not always been this small.

I almost lost Johnny this morning. That was her greatest fear, that she wouldn't be able to take care of her son. Tears, one by one, slid down her right cheek and refused to stop.

"Rosa," her grandmother whispered, "he is a boy. You cannot always be there. You must trust the Lord."

Rosa nodded, but one tear and then another dripped down her cheeks and then fell to the rough ground. Her grandmother spoke the bare truth; Rosa accepted that with her mind. But in her heart, she carried her son and her grandmother on her back alone. *Lord, please help me stop feeling this way. I know I can't guard Johnny from every danger. But, Lord, no more losing, please.*

Her eyes sought out Marc Chambers again. Opposite her and farther back in the crowd, he was standing close beside his grandmother who was looking up at him with stark anxiety on her face. Marc was rubbing his shoulder and rotating it as if in pain.

Then he looked up and his gaze connected with hers. She knew that harassed look, the "How much more can

I bear?" look. In fact, she had in the past looked into a mirror and seen it reflected in her own eyes. Her reaction was immediate. The urge to comfort to him swept over her.

Suddenly she recalled how disoriented Marc had been immediately after saving Johnny. She'd been in the midst of her own shock. Now she replayed the incident in her mind.

There was no reason for Marc to look so burdened by what had just happened. So this could not be about saving her son. What, then, had unnerved a brave man like Marc Chambers?

Two mornings later Marc stood at the open window of his apartment on the second floor of his grandmother's house. He watched the pink-gold of dawn finally gild the green fields that spread out on three sides of his grand-mother's house on Chambers Road. He had been waiting for dawn all night. He'd watched the predawn glow hover on the horizon for what had seemed hours and then the brightening had come. At last.

He rubbed his forehead. He hadn't slept at all the night before and not more than a couple of hours this night. Nightmares had kept waking him up. Each one had featured the screams and din from that awful day in January. He'd driven his semi onto the interstate; mist had iced the pavement. He'd lost control—a twenty vehicle pile-up, a fatal one. The intense sensations of that treacherous morning had tried to reclaim him, entrap him.

He leaned his forehead against the window frame. He had to begin again. He hadn't wanted to drive OTR—over the road—after that day. And he'd been recovering from injuries for months. Today, this was his challenge, and the night had depleted his fragile stamina.

He heard his grandmother, always an early riser, open her creaky back door to let her dogs out for their morning run. He turned to make himself a full "wake-me-up" pot of coffee.

God, I want this to stop. Haven't I been through enough?

His conscience didn't let him get away with this self-pity. *At least you're alive,* a voice in his head whispered, stabbing deep. He winced as if the pain were real. He tried to marshal his strength for this important new start. Why did the day have to start out like this?

Later, Rosa got out of her car and wrestled—once again—with the rusty, creaky door till she got it to shut properly. Embarrassed, she stared at the car. Like everything else she owned, it was on its feeble last leg. She looked around and took comfort that she wasn't the only one driving a decade-old, battered sedan.

Trying to distract herself, she looked around at the sun glinting on the community college campus's three buildings and large parking lot. *I can do this. I must.* Within her, the feeling of hope tried to bob to the top. But a growing case of nerves threatened to swallow that hope whole.

She pushed herself to start toward the nearest building, fighting the invisible force that was trying to drag her back to the car. Being here would naturally feel very strange at first, she told herself.

Resolutely, she headed in the direction indicated by the sign which announced Late Registration. Without warning, her fledging confidence and hope shriveled. Why had she thought she could do this, deserved this?

Late registration. She began to walk slower. *That's right—five years late registration. It would have been so different if I could have come here right after high school.*

Having Johnny in her senior year wouldn't have kept her from school, but...

Dark memories of long hospital days and nights at her mother's bedside, the smell of disinfectant and the sound of gurney wheels rolling nearby tried to suck her down into the past. *No.* She refused to allow the sadness to spoil this. She straightened her shoulders and marched with quick steps toward the entrance.

She entered the registration area in what must be a gymnasium. After blinking in the sudden dimness, she was able to survey her surroundings. There were three tables with signs posted above them, dividing the people who were registering into lines according to the alphabet.

She headed toward the *R-Z* table. As she passed the first two tables, she glimpsed someone she hadn't expected to see here. The man—he'd been called Marc—who had saved Johnny yesterday. An overwhelming reaction to seeing him startled her. He stood well ahead of her in the nearby *A-G* line. The sight of him dragged her back to the shock of seeing a cement truck bearing down on her son. It shot through her like an electrical charge.

She took a deep breath, forcing herself to calm down. But it didn't work. She couldn't take her eyes off him. If he turned and caught her staring, it would be embarrassing. And it wasn't just the memory of that awful moment; something about the man beckoned her.

It wasn't just that he was good-looking. Something about him spoke to her of diffidence. He looked like the kind of man who could handle anything, yet there was more there, something in the way he stood that spoke of tension and vulnerability, too.

Moving forward in her line, she hesitated to approach him. She sensed he wouldn't want her to make a big deal about his risking his life to save her son.

Yet the awareness of his being so near refused to go away. She forced herself to face forward; however, that didn't stop her from tracking him out of the corner of her eye.

As her registration line moved more rapidly than his, she reached the front, very aware of his standing just feet away. The woman manning the *R-Z* desk interrupted her preoccupation and asked for her name, checked a list and sent her to another line to have her student ID photo taken.

Rosa arrived there at the same moment Marc did. She took her rampant reaction into a firm grip and gave him a smile. "Hi, Marc."

"Hi, Rosa," he said, looking abruptly surprised. "I didn't know I'd be meeting you here."

Before she could reply, they were interrupted by the photographer. With an apologetic smile to her, Marc approached the photographer.

She watched Marc follow instructions to stand against what looked like an old projector screen and face the photographer. He wasn't dressed in jeans, but in khaki slacks and a dark green short sleeve shirt. He looked much more put together compared to the much younger students around them.

She studied Marc's face, a strong jaw, tanned skin. His face had filled out and firmed—so different from the teens laughing and talking around him. And though he was clean-shaven apart from the scraped skin, the outline of his beard was visible.

Marc didn't smile for the camera. Then his blue eyes captured her interest once again. They were underlined by dark gray smudges. That made her stop. What was causing him to lose sleep? She stared into those intense eyes. There it was again. That hunted impression. Her heart reached out to him.

Then the photographer called her to take her turn in front of the screen. Marc walked past her with a deprecating shrug as if apologizing for not being able to talk. Then still tracking Marc moving away, she tried to follow the photographer's too softly spoken instructions. After he had snapped her photo, she was told to go to another line where she'd get her photo.

She found this line and caught up to Marc. She gave him a cordial smile. Again she was too aware of this man. Normally, she would have spoken to him without self-consciousness. But something held her back. Was it the dark circles under his eyes? Or was this odd reaction completely due to the fact that *she* felt uncertain, didn't feel she belonged here? Was it all about her, not him?

"How's Johnny today?" he asked, glancing over his shoulder.

"Fine. He's home with my grandmother." *He's alive today because of you.* She did not say that thought out loud. He wouldn't appreciate her mentioning his heroic action yesterday. That much she knew about men like Marc. "This is my first time registering for classes here," she said, steering the conversation away from yesterday. "How about you?"

"Me, too."

Again, they were interrupted when he was called away by someone who read his name from a list. Again, he gave her a rueful smile and headed toward the person who was holding out a folder.

She picked up her ID and slipped it into her jeans pocket. Why did ID photos all seem to capture her with the classic "deer in the headlights" expression? It was not flattering.

Over an hour later, Rosa walked out of her counselor's office and nearly bumped into Marc, who was exiting the office on the opposite side of the hall.

"Oops," he said, "imagine running into you here." His tone was bright but his expression and posture spoke of exhaustion. Her immediate reaction was to help him.

"Let me buy you a cup of coffee in the student union," she offered, voicing her first thought of help. "I've never been there."

He hesitated only a moment. "Coffee. Sounds great." He motioned for her to lead the way.

Soon they were sitting across from each other at a long gray plastic and steel table. A young woman with waist-length red hair passed them, glancing markedly back at Marc. The redhead sat at a table several feet from them but in a position where she could watch them. Or was Rosa just imagining that? Just in case, Rosa glanced down, making sure that none of her buttons had come undone or anything else like that. The girl looked familiar. Who was she? *I know I know her.*

Turning toward Marc, Rosa blew over her steaming mug of creamy coffee. And wracked her brain for something neutral to talk about.

"What classes are you taking?" he asked, lifting his mug to his lips.

Well, that was certainly a neutral and a very natural question. She flipped open her folder and began reading aloud. "Composition, algebra—"

They were interrupted yet again. Shouting people were running into the union. Both she and Marc leaped from their seats.

A frantic sparrow flew over their heads, nearly grazing the top of Rosa's hair.

Unfortunately the union had a high industrial-style ceiling. The sparrow swooped to exposed metal rafters far above them. Rosa and Marc joined the growing crowd of mostly teens, all gawking upward as the distressed bird fluttered from beam to beam.

"We need to get it safely out of here," Marc said in a loud voice. He turned to the woman in charge of the nearby checkout station. "Call maintenance, will you? Tell them we'll need a ladder or two. And maybe some kind of net."

The young woman nodded and picked up a phone under the counter.

"Everyone needs to either leave or sit down," Marc suggested in a commanding tone. "A herd of gawking and squawking humans will keep the bird frantic. And harder to capture." Marc made downward motions with both hands. "Chill, birdwatchers."

There was a ripple of muted laughter and Rosa watched, startled, as a group of strangers followed Marc's direction. A few people left. Most sat and looked up, speaking rarely and in low tones.

This incident gave her another opportunity to take the measure of Marc Chambers. Yesterday plainly was not out of the ordinary for him. She'd heard of born leaders and here was one in action. He was a man who took charge in an emergency. She sat down where she could watch the unfolding nature drama.

Rosa noticed the young redhead girl was glancing up at the bird and then down at Marc. But then everyone was. Then two men in work clothing came in. Perhaps since Marc was the only one standing, they approached him. He pointed out the bird that was now fluttering along the ceiling looking for a way out.

The sound of the frantic wings and the frenzied chirping gave voice to the bird's agitation. They tugged at her emotions. It was just a little bird, but who couldn't identify with the feeling of being trapped?

"Can those high windows be opened?" Marc asked, pointing toward a bank of windows near the ceiling on one side.

"Sure. Sure," one of the workmen replied. Soon the two men set the ladders and busied themselves climbing and unlatching the high windows with long poles. When this was done, they rejoined the rest of the birdwatchers below. Marc returned to stand beside Rosa.

The union fell silent except for the bird's chirping. Rosa felt the urge to climb one of the ladders and shoo the bird toward freedom. Then it happened. The bird located an open window. With a joyful tweet, it flew outside to freedom.

Along with everyone else, Rosa jumped to her feet, applauding. She nearly threw her arms around Marc. A flash of consideration stopped her. But it didn't stop others who rose from their seats. As most left, they nodded or said something complimentary to Marc. He looked distinctly uncomfortable, just waving off the comments and trying to turn them aside with humor.

Rosa realized then that she would have to be careful around this man, the good man. Marc Chambers had managed to do something no man had done for years. *I am attracted to him.* This admission launched her fight-or-flight response. The urge to turn tail and bolt cascaded through her. She looked up at Marc. "I have to be going."

He nodded at her. "Sure. See you around."

She smiled even though her lips felt cold and tight. She headed straight for the nearest exit. *I don't want to be involved with anyone now. I shouldn't be. I can't be.*

Chapter Two

Outside, Rosa wrenched open her rusted and dented door and climbed into her car for the ride home. She plopped all her folders onto the seat beside her and put her hands on the wheel. Her body still buzzed with the fear of becoming captivated by Marc Chambers—by any man. It reignited all the emotional turmoil that had surrounded breaking up with Johnny's father only a month before her son's birth. How could the emotions from over five years ago still be so fresh, so raw, so powerful?

She closed her eyes, recalling the last argument with Trent. They had dated over a year and a half, but that day he'd shown her his real self, a self-centered and immature boy, who didn't want to be *saddled* with a kid. She silently prayed the twenty-third Psalm, a habit at times like these. Its phrases always calmed her. *Thy rod and thy staff comfort me...Surely goodness and mercy will follow me all the days of my life...*

Her breathing became normal again and her heartbeat, too. Opening her eyes, she started the car, checked her rearview mirror, and backed out of the parking spot. At home, she planned to sit down with a strong cup of coffee and study all the pages about everything from student parking to student activity fees. She would concentrate on what was really important *now*. No more past regrets. *This is real. I'm going back to school. At last!*

Several miles from school in the midst of the tall lush cornfields, Rosa drove around a bend. Red lights flashed and a bell rang ding-ding, ding-ding, sounding the warning. The barricade lowered over the railroad crossing. She rolled to a stop.

To keep her mind too busy for recurring thoughts of Marc, she lifted the folder, full to bursting with information that she'd been given at registration.

She laid out on the seat beside her all the papers she had been given and tried to put them in some order. Then she opened her purse and took out her wallet to put her student ID into one of the clear pockets.

She fingered her ID. It felt thicker than her driver's license. She looked at it more closely. Another laminated ID had become stuck to the back of hers. She separated the two and stared at the extra ID. The photo was of Marc Chambers who lived on Chambers Road.

Watching the final few freight cars pass by, she started her engine. The red flashing lights blinked out and the ding-ding sound stopped. The barricades lifted and Rosa drove, clattering over the metal and wood to the other side. To let the backed-up traffic pass, she pulled off onto the shoulder. Parked again, she looked over Marc's ID.

Marc Chambers lived on Chambers Road. That meant that his family had lived on their land before there had been a road. Then a glimmer of a memory of something about the Chambers family, something that had happened earlier this year, some tragedy earlier this year tried to come up in her mind. It eluded her. She looked around and realized what she had to do.

The Chambers' farm was closer than driving back to the

community college. And Marc might be back on campus before she would be and need his ID. Still it was hard to turn the car around and go toward him, the man she needed to start avoiding until she got over this…infatuation.

Maybe it was just all the new things in her life—the Habitat house, starting college—that had sparked her attraction to Marc. Perhaps when everything settled down again, her feelings would just dissipate on their own.

The few miles through the low, green potato fields and high cornfields passed quickly. Rosa slowed on Chambers Road. She paused to read the name on the first large gray mailbox. "Bud Tracy Luke Chambers." She decided that she should drive to the next house. There she found the mailbox that read Naomi Marc Chambers. In the distance, she saw Marc reclining in a lawn chair in the backyard. She drove in behind his truck, parked and cut her motor.

She climbed out of her car and walked over to him. That's when she noticed that he was sleeping. Those tell-tale gray smudges under his eyes worried her again. All alone, she took a moment to study him. The grazes on his face, wrist and hand were healing, dark red now instead of crimson. She stood in front of him, trying to decide whether to wake him or not.

The decision was made for her when he suddenly opened his eyes. He gazed at her for a moment and then said, "Rosa?"

"Sorry," she apologized and with a grin added, "I am not stalking you." She held out the ID. "I was halfway home when I realized I had your ID. Somehow it must have got stuck to the back of mine."

He got up politely and took the ID. He smiled. "Now I remember. I was called away to see my counselor before I got it."

"Yes, and you were right in front of me in line." The

fact that they were alone together for the first time did nothing to help her resist the pull toward him. She wanted to stay and just talk to him; therefore, she needed to leave as quickly as possible. She inched backward.

"I'm really sorry that you had to drive all the way here." He took out his wallet and tucked the ID inside.

"No problem. I can't stay," she said. "I'm waitressing at the Truck Stop tonight."

"Then I'm doubly sorry you had to drive over here," he replied, not giving her any information to explain his obvious fatigue.

They stopped talking and walking. For a breathless moment, they just stood looking at each other. The cicadas around them screeched. A tractor rumbled in the distance. The breeze rustled the cornfields around her. She didn't know what caused her to sense that something was bothering him, causing him to lose sleep.

Again, her mind tried to bring up the vague memory of what disaster had happened to the Chambers family earlier this year. *I've got to get going. I've just met this man, but already I've become sensitive to him, dangerously sensitive.* She took a large step backward and prepared to leave.

Marc tried not to yawn again. The lack of sleep must have caught up with him when he got home. He'd planned just to sit a moment and then sort through all the papers he'd lugged home. And now there was this pretty woman and he didn't want her to go and he didn't want her to stay. How weird was that?

His grandmother's dated station wagon groaned as it pulled into the drive and then parked beside Marc's pickup. Naomi got out and the opened the back door. Her two golden retrievers bounded out of the car, barking with their usual excitement. They quickly surrounded him and the woman who looked uncomfortable being there. He quickly waved the dogs away from her to him. "Rosa!" Naomi called out in greeting. "What brings you here?" Naomi asked, then scolded the dogs, who soon quieted.

Naomi asked, "Can we do something for you?"

"She brought me my student ID. Somehow it got left at the college." Marc hoped his grandmother wouldn't read anything into finding Rosa here.

"Well, come in, Rosa. I have iced tea in the fridge," Naomi invited, motioning toward the back door.

"No, thanks, I've got to get home. My grandmother is taking care of Johnny and I've got stuff to do before I go to work later," Rosa said and started walking toward her car.

"Thanks for bringing my ID to me!" Marc called after her.

He watched as she drove away, listening to the various rattles and groans her car made. It sounded like it needed work.

Naomi punched his arm. "So how did registration go?"

"Fine." He rubbed his arm, still sore from hitting the concrete on New Friends Street. Rosa's face came to mind and he remembered how concerned she'd looked earlier over the trapped bird.

"Marc," his grandmother said, sounding as if she were repeating his name.

"What? Do I need to carry anything in?" he asked, guessing.

"Yes, I bought some bags of dog food." She was studying his face.

Avoiding her astute eyes, he went along with her and opened the back hatch. *No matchmaking, please.*

"I'll go get the wheelbarrow—"

"No, I can carry fifty pounds." For months, however, he hadn't been able to lift anything because of broken bones from the accident. He was careful now to bend his knees and lift as the physical therapist had taught him. It felt good to be able to lift these bags again. He carried first one and then the other into the garage.

His grandmother hovered around him, chewing her lower lip and looking worried.

"I'm fine, Grandma. Fine."

"That Rosa is a very pretty girl—"

Before she could continue, his phone rang upstairs. *Saved by the bell.* He apologized to his grandmother and then ran up the stairs to his apartment. He answered the call on the sixth ring. "Hi."

"Marc," his brother Luke said, "Mom and Dad will be attending a Farm Bureau meeting next Thursday night. Meet me at the A & W at six for supper, okay?"

"Sure." Before Marc could say more, Luke hung up. Marc stared at his phone. What did Luke need to discuss with him away from the family?

Marc had slept for nearly four hours last night and he felt awake for the first time in days. Under the high morning sun over the Habitat site, he and a few other men, mostly retired, were setting the floor joists from the sill around the foundation to the center beam that would support the middle of the future floor of the house.

He'd not been eager to come for today's work at the Habitat site of Rosa's house. This place made him uneasy because this was where the near-accident had triggered the same nightmares and sleeplessness that had followed January's accident. But today—so far nothing. And perhaps a day spent working hard in the sunshine would make him fall asleep tonight, dreamless, and stay that way till morning.

He tried to concentrate on this simple job, but his eyes kept straying to Rosa and her son. Even wearing a red-and-white baseball cap, bright yellow work gloves and faded jeans, Rosa looked appealing and feminine.

She and his grandmother, Naomi, were carrying studs to be used for framing the walls. And Johnny was hanging around his grandmother who was sitting on a lawn chair in the shade of an old oak on the edge of the lot. A few stumps which would need to be cleared still edged the property. Fortunately whoever had excavated the basement had preserved some of the trees so the two of them were in the shade. Unfortunately Johnny looked depressed, unhappy.

Marc set the last of the floor joists into place, the web of support needed for the subfloor. Johnny was pushing a toy truck through what remained of the dirt pile left from the excavation that still needed to be trucked away. There was a pause while the men discussed how to lay the subfloor. Marc didn't join in.

He couldn't take his eyes from the poor kid. He still looked shamed and unhappy. Maybe he was remembering what had happened here a few days ago, the fear and the shame. Johnny's gloom worked its way inside Marc. Young spirits could be easily injured and that was never good. But what could he do about it? And should he?

After the day of the dedication with its near accident, he didn't want to call any more attention to himself. He turned back and concentrated on the discussion the men were having about how best to proceed. Marc knew how to proceed. But again, he didn't want to be disrespectful of the older men. He would wait until either they asked him for advice or were going to start in error.

Then Marc's grandmother walked past him. He glimpsed

the small hammer tucked into her belt loop and it gave him an idea. He resisted it. *Just let it go. He'll be fine.*

But Marc found that he couldn't stop himself. He couldn't stand by and not try to help the kid. Before coming today the boy obviously had been lectured not to do anything dangerous like he had the first day. The kid looked crushed and nobody should look that miserable.

Marc left the men and caught up with Naomi. "Grandma, let me borrow your hammer. It's just the right size."

Naomi glanced at him and then nodded.

He took the small hammer and went over to the building supplies area. He took a handful of short nails with broad heads and walked over to the boy. "Johnny, come here. I want to show you something." Marc waved toward the stump nearest to where the boy's grandmother was still knitting in the shade of the oak.

Marc knelt down on one knee and began sticking a few of the nails into the wide circle of the top of the stump. "Johnny, come here. You're old enough to learn how to pound a nail in place." This was how his own grandfather started to teach him basic carpentry. And this would give the kid something to do. Maybe it would even help him feel better.

Johnny walked slowly over. "What are you doing, mister?"

"Watch me." Marc used the small hammer to pound one of the nails into the stump. Then he handed the hammer to the boy. "Give it a try."

The boy looked at the hammer and then glanced back at his grandmother.

"Go ahead, Johnny," his grandmother coaxed in her melodic Spanish accent. "The man is right. A boy must learn to pound a nail. It is something men do. Your grandfather was a fine carpenter."

Johnny turned to face the stump. He hit one of the nails. It fell over. Crestfallen, Johnny looked at Marc in defeat.

"Hey, that's what happens to all of us the first time and many more. Here, I'll show you. You have to hold the hammer tight—like this. Okay?" Marc wrapped his hand over the boy's small one around the hammer's handle. He couldn't ever recall holding a child's hand. It gave Marc a funny feeling.

The feeling made him soften his voice another notch. "Now to pound in a nail—first you hit it square just to 'set' it." Marc demonstrated by gripping the small hand and hammer and hitting the nail just enough to get it started going in straight. "Then you give it another whack." Marc brought the hammer down with force, driving the nail half-way into the soft stump.

"Then we finish with one more stroke." Marc repeated the motion and the nail disappeared into the stump except for the nail head. "See? Three strokes does it."

Johnny looked sideways into Marc's eyes. "But I'm not as strong as you."

"This is how you become strong. Here, feel my arm." Marc moved his upper arm toward the boy.

Johnny squeezed it. "You are strong."

Again, the feel of the small hand somehow touched Marc's heart. "You will be, too, if you work at pounding nails. Now remember the first stroke, you set the nail. Just get it in enough so it won't wiggle. Then hit it straight on till you get it all the way in. Okay?"

Johnny had caught his lower lip with his front teeth. "Okay."

"Now you try it." Marc removed his hand, sat back on his heels and watched.

Johnny hit the nail and it went in just a bit, but straight.

"Good. Now the next stroke. Harder."

Johnny hit it again. It went in another fraction.

"Again—" Marc was interrupted.

"Hey, Chambers, we're ready to start laying the subfloor!"

Marc rose. "Just keep pounding them in. It takes a lot of practice. And here's how you pull the nails out." Marc demonstrated using the claw part of the hammer. "Pound them in and then pull them out and do it again. Keep practicing." Then he hurried away to join the men who were moving wood to lay the first layer of floor.

He passed Rosa. She was staring at him. And tears were in her eyes. That confused him. Why was she crying now?

Wondering why his brother had asked to meet him at A & W drive-in, Marc pulled into the parking lot. At the edge of town, A & W was the only fast-food place in Hope. For just a moment, he folded his arms on the steering wheel and rested his head there. He'd managed three hours of sleep last night—in between nightmares where he watched his eighteen-wheeler chew through cars, hearing the metal and screaming...

Wrenching himself back to the present, he got out, rubbing his face, trying to smooth out traces of fatigue. He went in to the line of booths on one side of the small eat-in area. His younger brother, Luke, was waiting for him in one.

Tempted by the fragrance of onion rings, Marc slid in the booth across from Luke. Before he could ask what this meeting was about, the high school-aged waitress, daughter of the owner, came to the table. Shyly, she greeted them by name and they gave her their order. Within minutes, his tall frosty mug of root beer arrived.

He took a long, cold, sweet swallow and then put down the heavy mug. "Okay, what's up?"

Luke stared at his mug on the orange plastic table. "You've got to promise not to laugh."

This struck Marc as very peculiar. And since he'd been asked not to laugh, he had to quell a grin. "Okay, I won't laugh."

Luke looked up like a turtle taking a peek out of his shell and then pulled back inside, looking down again. "I think I've finally found someone."

Marc did not act as if he didn't understand. Luke was unusually shy around girls—even when they had flocked around him when he played high school basketball. "That's good. Where did you meet her?"

"Online." Luke stared at the tabletop.

Stunned, Marc clutched the handle on his cold mug. "Wow."

"It's not what you think."

"I frankly don't have a thought about this," Marc said, "except how did you have the guts? I mean, did you sign up for one of those dating services?"

Luke nodded and didn't pull back into his shell. "I saw them advertised on TV. It's called GetLinked.com. You go online and set up a profile. Then they match you with people…you know, people who like the same things as you do."

"Where does she live?" Marc asked, intrigued out of his tiredness. "I mean, is this going to be a long-distance relationship?"

"No, it's so cool." Luke grinned with boyish eagerness. "I had a match in the Rhinelander." Luke grinned wider. "I like her already. She's really fun."

She's really fun. In his mind Marc heard Rosa's applause

when the bird flew free. He forced his mind back to Luke. "Have you met her?"

Luke didn't answer right away. He started playing with his paper napkin, moving it around the tabletop. "That's what I wanted to talk to you about. She wants to meet me but you know there are online predators, dangerous people."

Luke made eye contact. "Her...father will meet us there to see if he'll let her stay for the date."

"So what do you want from me?" Marc asked with rampant suspicion.

Luke looked suddenly uncertain again. "Well, with her dad coming to meet me she asked would my dad come, too. So the families would both get to see each other."

"Oh." Marc saw at once that Luke didn't want their parents in on this at all, not at this delicate point. Their mom would be all over it. She'd been hinting about grandkids for a few years now. It would be too much pressure for any girl and Luke needed space.

"So...I mean you're family.... So I want you to go on a double date with me and Jill." His brother stuttered over the lady's one syllable name and flushed bright red.

Double date? That implied Marc had to come up with a date. He hadn't dated for almost a year now. And he didn't want to—not now. Not till he felt like himself again. Not till he could think of Caroline without feeling guilty. But one look at Luke's pleading eyes and Marc was sunk. He nodded his agreement.

On Sunday afternoon, Rosa reluctantly drove the last mile to the farmhouse that belonged to Naomi, who had invited Consuela to her kitchen so they could can salsa together this afternoon. Rosa did not want to come along, but Consuela didn't drive. And how could she tell her grandmother that she didn't want to get closer to the Chambers family, especially Marc Chambers?

The fact that she was attracted to Marc meant that she should be putting distance between them, not driving right up to his door. The other day at the Habitat site, he had nearly melted her heart. She would never forget his helping her son learn to hammer in a nail. He was a good man and in some way a troubled man. How did she put those together? What didn't she know about him?

Consuela sat beside her, clutching a bag of small green jalapenos, which she grew in a large clay pot outside their apartment door. "I really like Naomi," Consuela said. "I can tell she has a good heart."

"I like Marc," Johnny piped up from the backseat.

I like Marc, too, Rosa's mind echoed. *And I don't want to.*

Consuela looked over her shoulder. "*Mi hijo,* Marc has a good heart, too, but you will play in the backyard. Senora Naomi says she has two dogs that you can play catch with. We will be busy canning the salsa."

"Yes," Rosa said, without betraying any of the turmoil she was feeling about coming to this place. *I'll just sit and read while Johnny plays.* "Johnny, I expect you to mind your manners. You are not to call Naomi by her first name. You call her Mrs. Chambers."

"*Si,* Mama." Johnny sounded bored by her instructions.

Rosa decided to let it go. Johnny had also begun school this week and had already brought home two papers with complimentary comments. He deserved an afternoon of playing with dogs. She drove up, crunching over the long gravel drive and parked in front of the detached white garage. Maybe Marc wouldn't be home. *What if he is? How can you stop Johnny from liking a man who is good to him?* Rosa had absolutely no answer for herself. She was in the same difficult situation.

No doubt alerted by her dogs barking, Naomi walked out her back door and waved to them. "Come on in!"

Sitting by one of the windows in his upstairs apartment, Marc heard his grandmother calling and looked outside. Rosa, Johnny and Consuela were climbing out of her battered blue sedan. The bright sunlight glinted on Rosa's silver-and-turquoise necklace and bracelet. In a red cotton shirt and worn jeans, she managed to look prettier than the law should allow a woman to look.

Below, his grandmother silenced the retrievers with a "Hush!" He made himself look back at his textbook—not out the window. *I will read and make sense of this.*

The voices still floated up to him, tantalizing. He didn't want to be sitting in here on a sunny day.

"Marc!" his grandmother called up. "Marc, can you come down here?"

Marc told himself that he should just go down for a moment to be polite and then come right back up here and study. With his book in hand, he headed down the flight of steps to the backyard. His tired heart thudded with the exertion and with the crosscurrents of wanting to come down and wanting not to. Luke's request that he find a date made his temples throb.

"Thanks, Marc," Naomi said with a brilliant smile. "Can you two watch Johnny so Consuela and I don't spoil the salsa because of interruptions?" Without waiting for a reply, both older women turned and disappeared into the kitchen.

Marc stood facing Rosa, still holding his textbook. He tried to think of words to say that would politely get him back upstairs studying. But all he could think was that her brown eyes were sober and somehow more striking because of their serious expression.

Rosa Santos was a very, very pretty lady. And the fact that she was raising Johnny alone tugged at his concern. Then the memory that he needed a date bumped and bounced in his mind, trying to get him to ask Rosa. *No, Rosa doesn't need me in her life. And I'm not over this second round of sleeplessness and nightmares.*

The doctor had called it post-traumatic shock. *But it went away. I got over it.* His subconscious taunted, *Really?*

"Hey, Marc," Johnny said, bouncing on his toes. "The dogs are barking. Can I let them out to play with me?"

"Sure. Sure." Marc pulled himself out his preoccupation. He sensed Rosa keeping her distance from him. Had she noticed his fatigue, his being distracted? Or was she as gun-shy as he was about getting close to someone of the opposite sex? "Come on."

"What are their names?" Johnny asked, running to keep up with Marc.

"Roxie and Dottie. Dottie's just a pup," Marc answered. Rosa's nearness prompted him to think about Luke's request again. Every time he thought of asking someone for a date, this woman came to mind. *No, I can't and for so many reasons.* "The dogs will love it if you throw the Frisbee so they can catch it," he said to Johnny.

Marc unlatched the gate to the dog run. The two golden retrievers bounded out, barking joyously and leaping up to lick Marc's nose and Johnny's face.

Raising his arms, Johnny covered his face as the dogs leaped higher than his head. "Help!"

"Down! Sit!" Marc ordered. Roxie who was nearly ten obeyed immediately but Dottie, the pup, had to be told several times. Finally, she sat.

In the sudden silence, Marc heard the tail of Rosa's gasp of alarm.

"They can…jump high," Johnny said, sounding out of breath and slowly lowering the elbows he'd raised to protect himself.

"Yes, they can—" Marc kept his tone even to bolster Johnny's confidence around the dogs and reassure Rosa "—but they are very gentle dogs and love to play."

Johnny eyed the dogs. "Okay. Where's the Frisbee?"

At the word Frisbee, Dottie leaped up and ran back into the dog run and returned with a chewed-up white Frisbee. She dropped it at the boy's feet and panted with anticipation.

"He brought it!" Johnny jumped up and down.

"*She* brought it," Marc corrected.

Johnny reached for the Frisbee but Dottie couldn't resist washing the boy's face with her eager tongue. "Sit!" Johnny yelled. "Sit!"

Rosa hurried closer. "Maybe these dogs aren't used to children—"

The fear in her voice washed over Marc. "Down, Dottie," he ordered, his tone fierce.

Dottie dropped to the ground and whimpered in a pathetic wounded tone. Johnny dropped to his knees and petted Dottie's head. "It's okay. Don't cry." Dottie stared up at him with imploring brown eyes and crept the few inches on her belly to him. She whimpered again.

Marc felt ashamed at scolding the dog so harshly. She didn't deserve it.

"It's okay," Johnny said, still petting Dottie. "It's okay, Dottie." She moved even closer, laying her head on Johnny's lap. The dog made one of those ridiculous sounds of pleasure, a cross between a sigh and a snort.

Marc smiled, suddenly feeling lighter.

Rosa chuckled. "Are you okay then, son?"

Marc turned and the expression on Rosa's lovely face snared him. Usually serious, her face now glowed with joy, a mother's joy. Marc's throat tightened. Suddenly he wanted to give her more reasons for joy. He wanted to help her with Johnny. *Stop. I can't be thinking this stuff. I've just been so lonely. That's why I'm having these thoughts.*

Johnny laughed. The older dog, Roxie, sidled up to Johnny and nudged his other hand. The little guy smiled and began petting both dogs with each hand. "What kind of dogs are these, Marc?"

"Mr. Chambers," Rosa corrected.

"Uh-huh," Johnny agreed.

"These are golden retrievers. They are very good with children. They like to play. They were originally bred for hunting. So they like to run."

"Another thing that boys like to do too," Rosa added with a grin in her voice.

That drew Marc. He turned to her. The same smile lit her face and he wanted to touch that face, feel the warmth of the radiance.

"I think I want this kind of dog when our house is built," Johnny said.

"You might want to go to the animal shelter," Marc said, "and pick up a dog that needs a home." This simple exchange had moved him, calmed him. The urge to touch Rosa's cheek now became irresistible. He raised his hand, reaching for her.

But then Marc dropped his arm. Touching Rosa would be inappropriate. He hated that he was not acting like himself. This had all been triggered the day Johnny had run in front of the cement truck. When would he start feeling like himself again?

Rosa tilted her head, looking at him questioningly.

He had no answer for her, but her effect on him was unmistakable. His mouth had gone dry and there was a knot in his chest.

She broke the connection. She reached for the Frisbee on the ground and tossed it. The dogs raced to catch it. Johnny shouted encouragement, bouncing after them several feet away. Again, Rosa stared into his eyes as if searching for something. "What is it, Marc?" she whispered.

"Hey!" a voice hailed them, interrupting Rosa.

Marc looked over her head at Luke walking up the drive toward them. Marc closed his eyes and thought how much easier it would have been if he'd just stayed upstairs.

Luke was grinning broadly.

Oh, no, Luke, this isn't what you might be thinking, bro. Before Marc could put the words together, Luke stuck out his hand to Rosa. "Am I glad to see you. Rosa Santos, right? We went to high school together."

"I am Rosa," she said, taking his hand but looking to Marc.

"Yeah, I know," Luke said. "I didn't know you and Marc knew each other."

"This is my brother, Luke," Marc managed to get out.

"Oh." Rosa's eyes widened. "That's right. You're Luke Chambers. We did go to school together. You were on the state championship basketball team."

"Yeah," Luke said and let go of her hand. "That must be your little boy. He turned out to be a pretty sturdy little guy. He might be good at sports."

"Thank you. I think he's kind of special."

Johnny turned and said something to his mom. Rosa moved away a few paces to answer his question.

Luke sidled over and said in a low tone, "I hope you have enough sense to ask her out. Rosa Santos. I could never understand why Johnny's father didn't marry her. I mean, after they finished high school, that is. She was one of the prettiest and sweetest girls on the cheerleading squad. I'd lost track of her."

"She's here because her grandmother's inside with Naomi canning salsa," Marc said, feeling desperate to head Luke off. "I'm just helping build her house in town. That's *all*."

Luke ignored the last sentence. "Oh, the Habitat house. Mom was talking about that but I didn't pay much attention. Maybe I should come help out too? And Dad." Luke lowered his voice another notch. "Anyway, Jill is starting to think I'm a loser who doesn't have a family or I'm trying to get out of meeting her. If you're not asking Rosa out, then you better come up with somebody fast for the double date. I don't want to lose Jill."

"I just…I haven't dated lately." Unable to say more, Marc hoped Rosa hadn't overheard Luke talking about her. His brother hadn't said anything that he shouldn't—except the part about Marc asking Rosa out. Maybe if he avoided Rosa and Johnny, everything in his head would go back to normal. It was worth a try. But after the past few days, he had a feeling that no matter how hard he tried that avoiding Rosa would turn out impossible.

Chapter Three

In the campus library, Rosa sat across from the man she was trying to avoid—with extremely limited success—Marc. A few minutes ago they had been sitting in their first class together. How could she have known that Marc would be taking Introduction to Law Enforcement Careers, too?

"Well, I guess we should get started?" he said in a false hearty tone.

She forced a fake smile and nodded.

"Why don't we do you first?" he asked.

At that moment, outside the nearby wall of windows, a cloud shifted, letting a shaft of brilliant sunlight cast itself onto Marc's hair. The reddish highlights there shimmered like bright unseasoned copper. The breath caught in her throat. She stiffened her resistance. *This silly crush will pass. And soon.* She peddled down her reaction. "Okay." A little word hiding so much inside.

"Why did you decide to take this class?" he read from the interview page they'd been given to fill out. He had his pen poised to write down her answer.

Why did teachers do this? Make them do assignments together. What was this, high school again? That was an unfortunate thought. High school and its immediate aftermath had been the worst years of her life. "When I was in middle school," she began, forging on, "I was in the Big Sisters program." She took a breath. Why did being near Marc make it hard for her to breathe?

He nodded, encouraging her.

"The woman who was my Big Sister for three years worked in the state trooper's office as a dispatcher. She was a…real role model for me. That's why I chose law enforcement." Rosa nearly sighed with relief.

As Marc was writing, Rosa saw movement from the corner of her eye. Someone who was standing almost out of her line of peripheral vision had caught her attention. The person was just standing and watching them. Why?

"Is that all?" Mark asked, sounding like he wanted her to have much more to say. That was odd.

She turned her attention back to him. The insight struck her that each of them was peering at each other from behind masks. She was hiding her deep sorrow and regrets. What was he hiding? "That's all, I'm afraid. Your turn."

Marc cleared his throat.

She waited with her pen poised. Then from the corner of her eye, she saw that the person who was watching them had stepped into her line of sight. It was that girl she'd seen in the student union that day of the trapped bird. She realized now that this young woman had been in high school with her, not in the same year though. What was her name and why did she find Rosa interesting? Or maybe it was Marc. He was a man worth looking at after all.

She looked back to Marc. From his studied expression, she guessed that he was trying to figure out how little he could get by with telling her. What was Marc trying to conceal?

Marc started speaking fast. "I was an Over the Road

driver for nearly ten years. I had an accident and decided I didn't want to live that lonely life anymore. I was impressed by the emergency staff that responded to the accident in January. And that's why I'm here."

Suddenly several things happened at once in Rosa's mind. Marc's mention of an accident in January broke the dam, which had been holding her back from remembering. She knew which accident he was speaking about. In January there had been a horrible chain reaction highway accident, south on the interstate around Madison. Many people had been injured and a few died. It had been on the local TV news for over a week. Marc had been mentioned and also…

The name of the girl watching them came to Rosa. She was Penny Mason. And Penny's older sister, who had been living near Madison, had been killed in that January accident. What was her name?

Rosa realized that her mouth was hanging open. She closed it. This prevented her from blurting out all that she had just connected together. She throttled the desire to say anything about the accident. Now she knew a bit of what made Marc protect his privacy. Maybe he was just tired of people asking about the accident, talking about it.

She read the next question on the sheet. "What particular field of law enforcement are you interested in now?"

"I don't know really. That's why I'm taking this course. I just want to be able to help people…" His voice trailed off.

She nodded, still keeping her lips together.

"What about you?" he asked.

Penny Mason distracted Rosa by moving away, running away. The young woman's pace quickened the closer she got to the exit.

Marc must have noted the direction of her gaze. He started to turn his head toward Penny.

No. Rosa grabbed Marc's hand that rested on the top of the table. That swung his gaze back to her—as she had hoped. But now she had to come up with a logical reason for touching him. "I need to apologize," she said. "I couldn't help overhearing your conversation with your brother that afternoon in your backyard." She blushed, recalling that Luke had called her pretty and urged Marc to "ask" her. She plunged on, "Who are you going to ask for the double date?" She blushed hotly.

Marc stared at her.

She took a deep breath. "Sorry. I didn't mean to stick my nose into your business."

Marc sat back, pulling his hand free. "I haven't asked anyone. I haven't dated for a while." His face hardened somehow as if fighting pain.

Sympathy rushed through her. He must have spent months recovering from his injuries from the accident. "Me neither."

A slideshow of images of her son and Marc together flashed through her mind. *No, don't,* she ordered herself. *Stop.* But her mouth couldn't stop the words that had welled up from deep inside. "I could go with you—just as friends."

He gazed at her and then swallowed. "Thanks. I don't want to let Luke down. We *could* go just as friends."

She heard more than his simple words. He was fearful of her getting the wrong idea. He wasn't ready to date and neither was she. At least, that was what she always told herself when her mind drifted to Marc.

Her face still blazed over what she had just done. She wondered exactly what shade of red her face had turned.

But this wasn't about her. It was about helping Marc who deserved her assistance. But a date?

That was tricky. She would have to be very careful not to let on that she thought about Marc often. Way too often. *Lord, help me go on this date and yet keep a sensible distance.* But what was a sensible distance?

On Tuesday evening, Rosa waited by her car which she had parked in front of her half-built house. It was the evening she was supposed to double date with Marc—just as a friend. But why then was she wearing her best dark wash jeans, her favorite red blouse and an embroidered jean jacket?

This is not a real date, she reminded herself. Nonetheless, it was troubling to realize that no matter how much she said this to herself, she had been unable to stop herself from both dreading and looking forward to this evening.

She heard Marc's pickup before she saw it. And that gave her pause. When had her hearing tucked away the sound memory of Marc's truck? This could not be good.

Marc parked in front of her and got out of his truck. He beat her to his passenger side door and opened it for her.

"You didn't need to do that," she murmured, surprised and pleased. So few men today showed such courtesy.

"Glad you didn't bite my head off," he said with almost a grin. "I've tried to open doors for a few women and they've nearly mowed me down."

She reached up and grabbed the hand hold and lifted herself onto the high seat. "Some women think the old courtesies are demeaning, but I can be a liberated woman and still appreciate kindness." *And you are a kind man, Marc Chambers.* This thought tugged her heart. *Keeping my distance would be so much easier, Marc, if you weren't so kind.*

"Glad to hear that. My grandmother always says that she didn't need women's lib—she was born liberated." He shut her door and hurried around and got in.

Rosa smiled at his comment. "Your grandmother is quite a woman. I hope that I can face turning eighty with as much zest as she is."

Marc fell silent. He was looking at the street and tapping his hand on the steering wheel.

Rosa turned to study his expression. He looked pained. Learning about the accident was only part of the puzzle that was this complex man. There was more she was sure, perhaps something about Penny Mason's older sister. She thought the older sister would have been in high school when Marc was.

"Here's Luke," Marc said, sounding relieved.

"Oh, I wondered where he was," Rosa said, not admitting that when Marc had arrived, she had totally forgotten Luke. This was not a good sign.

Luke parked his truck in front of Marc's and walked to the pickup and climbed onto the seat beside Rosa. "Hi," he greeted her with a shy smile.

"Hi, Luke." Now she was sitting very close to Marc and trying not to touch him. She wondered what her future neighbors—the few that already lived at the end of the New Friends Street—thought of her going off with two men.

"We didn't want our family to know we were going somewhere together," Marc supplied the explanation of this rendezvous point.

"Yeah," Luke said, sounding embarrassed, "I know it sounds funny that we want to keep this quiet like a couple of teenagers—"

"No, I understand completely," Rosa said quickly. If she were in Luke's position, she wouldn't want her grandmother to know that she was going off to meet someone from an online dating service.

"Great," Luke said with obvious relief.

Marc was driving them north out of town toward Rhinelander. Silence developed and Rosa knew that if she didn't break it, it wouldn't be broken. "Luke," she started, "how long have you and Jill been in contact over the Internet?"

"About three months online and...and then I asked her in June if I could call her and talk on the phone. So we've talked several evenings for hours. I had to get more minutes on my cell phone." He sounded as if he'd been running and he had to stop to get his breath.

The information was mundane, but Luke's tone of voice told more than the words. Luke was very interested in this woman and very hopeful. Rosa sighed silently. She hoped that this Jill would be what Luke hoped for.

Though silent and seeming tense, Marc drove as if he knew where he was going. Soon he pulled into a parking lot of a family restaurant where Rosa and her family had eaten at often over the years. "Oh, the Diner. I love their fried chicken."

"So does Jill," Luke said, sounding relieved and nervous at the same time.

Rosa let Marc help her down from the truck. The three of them walked toward the entrance. An older man in a well-pressed shirt and dark dress slacks and a young woman, a petite blonde in jeans and a ruffled white shirt, waited just inside the door. There was a pregnant pause while they all stared at each other.

"Jill?" Luke asked, managing to stutter over the one syllable name.

Jill beamed. "Hi, Luke. Yeah, I'm Jill." She looked up at the man beside her. "This is my dad, Tom Bellers."

Tom held out his hand to Luke who shook it but he didn't take his gaze from Jill. In fact, their gazes locked and held.

"And who are these people, Luke?" Tom prompted, not unkindly.

Luke looked startled.

Marc held out his hand. "I'm Luke's brother, Marc, and this is my date, Rosa Santos. Rosa and I attend community college together."

Rosa was pleased with Marc's unexpected aplomb in this awkward situation.

"Can I see some ID?" Tom asked.

Jill blushed. "Dad, you know that Luke was investigated by the dating service—"

"I'm not leaving my little girl with strangers without proper ID," her father said.

Both Luke and Marc showed Tom their driver's licenses and auto insurance cards. Rosa began talking to Jill to help the young woman over this embarrassing moment.

"Okay. I checked several public sources about you, Luke, and you don't have a criminal record or anything else unsavory that I could find. I was going to stay here in the restaurant and sit at a different table. But now that I see you I don't think I'll have to do that. But Jill, remember that you aren't to ride anywhere with them or go into any private place, right?"

Jill looked pained but replied without any tinge of rudeness. "Yes, Dad."

"I will expect to meet Jill and the three of you back here by closing. Where are you all going after supper?"

Luke spoke up, "The bowling alley is just a few blocks away. I thought that would be best. We can just walk there."

"That meets with my approval." Tom leaned over and

kissed his daughter's forehead. "Have a nice evening, honey." And then he waved and departed.

"I'm sorry," Jill said. "My dad is kind of protective of me. There's only been the two of us since Mom passed away a year ago."

"I'm so sorry to hear that," Rosa said, truly touched. "My mother passed away three years ago." *And I never knew my father.*

"Oh, I'm sorry." Jill sent Rosa an understanding look.

Rosa nodded, wondering if Jill knew how lucky she was to have a dad who cared enough to protect her.

"Well, shouldn't we go in?" Luke suggested, gesturing toward the inner door.

Jill nodded. And Rosa was grateful. She didn't want to discuss losing mothers. Or fathers.

Luke ushered Jill into the restaurant while Rosa preceded Marc inside. The diner was filled with happy people eating good food. The group mood lightened as they slipped into the high dark wood booth the hostess showed them to. They sat as two couples. Rosa was more sensitive than ever of Marc sitting so close to her. Waves of awareness washed over her.

Rosa only glanced at the menu, already knowing that she would order her favorites. She noticed that Jill had also barely glanced at the menu.

"We come here a lot of Sundays after church," Jill explained in reply to Rosa's unasked question.

"Really?" Luke asked. "That sounds like something I'd like to do. I mean go to…church with you and then come here," Luke stuttered.

Jill beamed at him. "I'll tell Dad. He'll like that."

"Thanks for doing this," Marc murmured close to Rosa's ear.

His warm breath on her sensitive flesh made her tingle.

She smiled in response and sat back against the booth, ready to enjoy this carefree evening. She hadn't dated since high school—too busy and too cautious. This wasn't a real date, she reminded herself.

But she liked sitting next to Marc Chambers in this booth, having him near soothed some inner rawness she had barely been aware of before this moment. *I could get used to this very easily.* Inner warnings bells rang. She ignored them.

I'm just going to enjoy this evening as a double date. That's all. I'm entitled to a date once every five years. That thought nearly ruined her mood, but she pasted a smile on her face and gave her order to the waitress. "Fried chicken dinner please, corn on the cob, mashed potatoes, and a salad with French dressing." Good food, good company— what more could she ask for?

One glance at Marc's profile and her mouth went dry. And even though this wasn't a real date, it suddenly felt like one. And Rosa couldn't find the strength to stop her pleasure at sitting next to a man like Marc Chambers. More than one appreciative glance had come his way. *Just tonight—with Luke and Jill—that's all this is about.*

The bowling alley was noisy in a cheerful "let's have fun" spirit that Rosa found contagious. It had worked on Jill and Luke, loosening them into talking more and acting more natural. Rosa sat at their booth and watched Luke show Jill how to get a better hold on the bowling ball. Bursts of laughter and falling pins punctuated her good mood.

Marc leaned over and murmured into her ear, "From Jill's score, I don't think for a moment that she needs any instruction."

Rosa chuckled and nodded. Wonderfully relaxed, she

noticed that Marc had become more at ease, too. Maybe the bowling alley had done its magic on them, too. Then she chuckled to herself thinking of the phrase, "bowling alley magic."

"What's so funny?" Marc asked.

She shook her head, holding in the glee of the moment. Then she realized that this was not helping her intention of keeping her distance from Marc. That being near Marc could be a big part of her high spirits. Recklessly she studied his profile—the curve of his ear, the tan that gave his face a healthy glow, the five o'clock shadow on his jaw.

Jill made a strike and Luke gave her a high five. Then the two came back to the booth. "It's time we started back to the restaurant." Jill looked at her watch. "The Diner will be closing soon."

Rosa and Marc rose and the four of them went through the ritual of turning in shoes and heading out into the dark summer night. There was a hint of rain in the air. Rosa sniffed it in deeply and hoped that they would get a shower—after she got home.

They reached the Diner and met Jill's father at the entrance. "Well," Jill said, holding out her hand to Luke, "I had a lovely time tonight. And it was so good meeting you, too, Marc and Rosa."

Luke took her hand and stammered, "I really enjoyed seeing you. I'll call you, all right?"

Jill waved as she walked away.

Rosa watched the young, obviously shy, couple with a sense of sadness. She realized that Jill was not much younger than herself. Yet, she, a single mom, felt a thousand years older. Rosa walked between the two brothers to the truck.

No one said anything till they reached New Friends

Street. Luke was walking to his truck when he said, "Thanks a lot, both of you. Thanks."

"You're welcome," Rosa called in return. To Marc, she said, "Thanks for a fun evening." She found she couldn't say more without revealing more about her feelings for him. So she just smiled and walked toward her car.

"I owe you. Thanks." Of course, he began escorting her to her sedan.

Rosa stopped and looked around. What had she heard? She strained and heard it again—a whimper. Something was in pain and was imploring her for help. She gripped Marc's sleeve. "Did you hear that?"

It came again. The heartrending sound was coming from her partially built house.

"I hear it," Marc whispered, looking into the lengthening shadows of deep dusk.

"I'm going to find out what it is." She nodded toward the shell of her house, toward the sound.

"Walk slow," Marc said. "I'll get my flashlight."

The whimpering increased as she approached the shell. She looked down into the foundation and saw the outline of a dog, lying under the crude open stairway into the basement. When the animal saw her above, it whimpered louder still, begging for help. The sound stabbed her heart. She hurried carefully down the open stairs to the basement.

"If he's hurt, don't get too close," Marc cautioned, arriving just behind Rosa and switching on a large lantern flashlight.

She knew what he said was true, but then the poor dog inched toward her, whimpering, asking for help. "He's hurt and he isn't behaving snappish. I think he wants us to help him."

"Does he have a collar?" Marc asked.

"No." Rosa studied the animal by the light Marc

provided. "I wonder if he was the stray Johnny ran after into the street."

"Might be."

She stooped near the dog. "I think his front paw is swollen."

"That looks right," he agreed.

"We need to help him," Rosa said. "Marc, will you pick him up?"

Marc hesitated. A wounded stray might bite. But then three things happened. It began to sprinkle on the subfloor above them. Rosa looked up to him with a pleading look in her eyes. And the dog licked her hand. The final act made his decision. Marc stooped beside Rosa. "Tell him it's okay and pet his head. Tell him to let me pick him up."

She stroked the dog's head and murmured, "Marc is a good guy. He's going to lift you up and we're going to help you."

Finally, Marc put down the lantern flashlight, moved forward, and slid both arms under the dog. He lifted the dog up slowly. The animal closed its eyes as if releasing his troubles to them. "He's really light, undernourished. I think he must be a stray."

"Poor thing," Rosa murmured and picked up the lantern.

The injured dog was so pathetic, so helpless, Marc choked up. He knew what that felt like. He, too, had lain, injured, in pain and dependent upon the help of strangers.

"Do you know a vet who works this late?" she asked.

Marc considered the options. The dog moaned as if urging Marc to make up his mind already. "Let's take him to my grandmother. We usually have her look at our animals before we call the vet. In her day, farmers tended their own animals unless it was something serious. She'll tell us if we can take care of it tonight or need to wake the vet for an emergency."

Rosa nodded. Under the light sprinkling, she led the way, shining the lantern on the ground so they wouldn't stumble over anything. Soon they were at Marc's truck. He laid the dog gently on the seat and then turned to say goodbye. "Thanks again, Rosa, for tonight."

"Will you let me know how he does?" she asked.

"Will do." He turned to get out of the light rain.

But as soon as Rosa began to walk away, the stray began a combination of pitiful barking and moaning. It was such a pathetic mournful sound that Mark couldn't ignore it.

And evidently not Rosa, either. She came back. "You'll be all right, *amigo*. Marc will take good care of you."

The pitiful barking and moaning increased in volume and appeal. Marc realized that he had only one course. He took a deep breath. "Okay, evidently he has bonded with you. How about I put him on your front seat and you follow me home? I know it's late but it won't take Gram long—"

"Okay, let's get going," she interrupted, glancing at her watch and holding her purse over her head to shield herself from the quickening rain.

Within moments, Marc was in his truck, driving toward home, Rosa's aging car in his rearview mirror. Soon he and Rosa drove up to the white garage. From the dog run, his grandmother's golden retrievers came out of their houses to bark at him, welcome him. Marc stared at his grandmother's house unhappily. He hadn't expected this.

He got out of his truck, light lukewarm rain falling on him. The high yard light illumined the scene. His grandmother's first-floor apartment was uncustomarily dark. It was too early for her to have gone to bed. Where could she be?

"What is it, Marc?" Rosa called from her open car door.

The fact that he was keeping Rosa here when she should be home in bed resting tightened his jaw. A single mom needed her sleep. "Gram must be out tonight." And then he remembered. "Square-dancing night," he said. Annoyed, he glanced at his watch. "Out later than usual."

"What do we do with our furry friend then?" From behind Rosa, the dog whimpered, moaned loud and long.

The agonizing sound knit Marc's neck muscles into tight knots. "Let's get him inside. Gram should be along any time now." Then the rain began to fall faster and harder. He hurried to Rosa's car, lifted the dog and then loped toward his Gram's back door.

Rosa jogged just behind him, holding a bright pink umbrella over the stray. They reached the locked door, rain splattering around their feet on the patch of concrete.

"The keys are in my right pocket," Marc said, nodding down toward his right side.

Rosa pulled out the key ring. He told her which key to use. The umbrella tilted and rain streamed down the back of his neck. The lock turned; they burst into the large combination mudroom and back stairwell of the farmhouse. Rosa switched on the overhead light near the door.

Blinking in the sudden brightness, he looked around for a place to lay the dog. "Rosa," he said, nodding toward a white metal cabinet, held shut by a wooden clothespin, "please look in there for vinyl picnic tablecloths."

Rosa quickly followed his instructions. She laid the rumpled red-and-white-checked vinyl cloth over the top large chest-style freezer. Marc gently laid the dog onto it. "Okay, boy, let's see if there's more than your paw that needs help." He looked to Rosa, appealing silently.

She nodded her understanding and moved to the dog's head, hovering there, crooning soft words, soothing the animal's fears. Marc's examination didn't take long. The dog was malnourished, slightly feverish and had an injured paw. Marc hadn't touched the paw. Nonetheless he had seen easily that it was lacerated and swollen with infection.

Outside the gentle shower intensified to a pounding downpour. Worse and worse. Marc stood back and propped his hands on his hips. "This looks fairly straightforward. We need to clean him up and then use an antiseptic on the paw. I'll have to take him to the vet tomorrow for a tetanus shot and maybe an antibiotic. But with some first aid, this can wait till morning."

The rain outside gushed from the downspouts, distracting him as he tried to think how to proceed. The filthy dog needed a bath first. Yet he didn't want to take the dog to his gram's bathtub without her permission or try to drag the stray upstairs.

As if reading his mind, Rosa suggested, "Why don't we just shampoo him outside? Warm rainwater is the best rinse."

Marc stared at her. "You'll get all wet."

"I'm already wet. Denim won't be ruined by rain. And this will actually be easier on our stray *amigo* here."

The rain hammered outdoors. "Okay. I'll carry him outside. If you look on the top shelf in the cabinet, there's some canine flea shampoo." He was already shoving the door open with his foot and shoulder. "Let's get this done. Fast."

Rosa watched Marc step out into the tropical-feeling deluge. He looked tired yet determined. She followed him out with the bottle of flea shampoo in her hand. Tepid, not cooling rain poured down on her head. She was instantly wet to the skin. With every step, water squished up around her feet. She pushed her wet hair back from her face, glad her mascara was waterproof.

In the driving summer rain, Marc wrapped his arms around the middle of the dog. Fortunately because within seconds, the dog made his objection to a bath—loud and forceful. He tried to wriggle free. He moaned. He yipped. He wiggled.

Nonetheless, Rosa lavishly poured on the medicinal-smelling shampoo and started scrubbing the dog from his nose to his tail. The smell of wet dog filled her head as her fingers dug deep through the matted fur to the hide covering the thin body. "Poor *amigo*," she repeated and repeated. Rain streamed down her face, saturating every inch of her hair and clothing.

She'd just finished the sudsing when the dog made one more valiant or lunatic attempt to break free. He tried to bolt and knocked them both off their feet. Marc landed beside her on the squishy grass, squirting up water. The impact forced the air from her. She turned to him and their noses brushed.

Everything began to move in slow motion.

He leaned closer, looking at her lips. Her breath caught in her throat. Shock waves shuddered through her. Marc drew her irresistibly. She leaned forward, unable to take her eyes from his lips, so near, so enticing.

The animal intervened. He barked indignantly and strained to get away from Marc's last-ditch hold on his hind leg. Then a car bumped its way up the drive.

Coming back to her right mind, Rosa rolled away from Marc. Staggering, she rose with the rain still pouring down on them as if she were standing directly under a sky-high faucet.

His grandmother's dogs began barking in greeting. And his grandmother got out of a friend's car and walked toward them. "What's all this?" Naomi asked, dressed in an embroidered jean dress and beaming at them from under a large black umbrella. "You both look like drowned rats."

Rosa stayed away from Marc, still breathing harder than normal. As she began walking beside Naomi under her umbrella to the back door, Rosa explained how they had found the stray. Behind them, she heard Marc scrambling, splashing, the dog barking and yowling. He hurried to catch up to them with the dog, carrying him through the door she held open for him.

He passed within a fraction of a breathless inch from her. Rosa tried to calm herself. That moment on the ground had been a close call. Had she actually almost let Marc Chambers kiss her?

Chapter Four

Feeling the dog nudge him, Marc awoke in his bed to morning light. He lay, letting memories of a few nights ago play through his mind again. Rosa and he had scrubbed a dog together in drenching rain. Rosa's thick dark hair had been pasted to her face and forehead as she had scrubbed the dog from stem to stern. She'd ended the evening by naming the stray Amigo, Spanish for *friend*.

He closed his eyes, trying—in vain—to blot out pleasant images of Rosa, her lively face, her squeals of laughter as the dog had tried to break away from them. How was he going to stop himself from having these thoughts he'd banned? At the community college, he'd steered clear of her the past two days, but today loomed—

Impatient, Amigo nudged him in the side and gave a minor bark, asking for breakfast no doubt. In the past two days, Amigo had made himself at home. He ignored the ancient dog bed Naomi had set up for him and insisted on sleeping beside Marc on the bed. An unforeseen blessing.

Over the past two nights with Amigo by his side, Marc had somehow gotten through each night with only a bare minimum of nightmares. Not perfect, but better. Maybe it would just take time.

Amigo barked in earnest this time, breakfast clearly on his mind.

So Marc rolled toward the dog beside the bed. He rubbed his knuckles on top of Amigo's head and grinned in friendly amusement at the sight of the dog. Around the dog's neck was a silly but needed contraption that sort of looked like a satellite dish. It was necessary to keep the dog from chewing at the bandage on his one paw. The morning after the memorable doggy bath, Rosa had called to find out what the vet had said. Marc recalled hearing her soft voice on the phone, a pleasure.

Marc had reported that the vet had established that the dog did not have Lyme's disease, but was malnourished and needed antibiotic and vitamin pills daily. Amigo had been given both tetanus and anti-rabies shots. The vet bill had been a hefty one for a stray, but Marc realized that Amigo had come to stay. Once more he knuckled the top of the dog's head vigorously and Amigo looked pleased. "How are you feeling today, you worthless dog?"

Amigo barked, as if appreciating the dubious compliment. He barked again more insistently.

"Okay, okay," Marc said, rolling out of bed. "You're right. It's time for your breakfast." Marc stumbled to the kitchenette and opened a large can of dog food. He buried the morning antibiotic and vitamin pills in it, plopped the food in a bowl and set it down. He counted the remaining antibiotic pills to make sure he hadn't missed one. He hadn't. *Good.*

As he watched the dog inhale breakfast, more thoughts of Rosa flickered through his consciousness. That moment the other night in the midst of the deluge—their noses had touched. He'd nearly kissed her. *What was I thinking?*

The answer, of course, was that he was not thinking—just reacting to a pretty and very caring lady being so close. *Stop.* The command continued to have no effect. Rosa refused to be ousted from his mind. Marc went to the bathroom to get ready for the day—another day at the Habitat site, another day of temptation to draw closer to Rosa. *I will just do my work and stick to myself.*

Later that morning, he and his grandmother Naomi arrived at the Habitat site on New Friends Street. Marc's intention to steer clear of Johnny and Rosa as politely as possible was set in concrete.

From the corner of his eye, he watched Rosa drive up in her beat-up car. She, her grandmother, and of course, Johnny got out. Johnny was carrying the small hammer and a dilapidated paper bag which Marc supposed held nails.

"Hi! Mr. Chambers!" Johnny called out, waving the hammer Naomi had let him keep.

Marc glanced at him, smiled and saluted. He stood among the volunteers gathered for the opening prayer. At the "amen," the cheerful hubbub of people who were becoming friends blossomed around him.

Eleanor Washburn, the woman who was in charge, approached him with a young woman with long golden brown hair pulled into a pony tail tagging along.

"Jeannie Broussard," Eleanor said, "this is Marc Chambers. Marc—Jeannie."

Marc wondered why Eleanor was introducing them. So after shaking Jeannie's hand, he waited.

"Jeannie has just been approved to receive the second Habitat house here on New Friends Street on the next lot." Eleanor nodded toward the vacant lot next to Rosa's corner one. "What am I thinking?" She tapped her forehead.

"Rosa!" She glanced around. "Rosa, will you come here, please?"

Marc tried to hide the fact that his jaw had just clenched. What was Eleanor up to?

Rosa came, eyeing the group warily.

Eleanor repeated what she'd just said to Marc and then introduced the two women.

"I see you have a little boy," Jeannie said shyly, motioning toward Johnny. "I have twin girls just about his same age."

Rosa smiled. "Great. Then our kids won't have to go far to find playmates."

Marc hooked his thumbs in his jeans belt loops and wondered where this was leading. Then Eleanor fixed her gaze on him. "Your grandmother tells me that you are an experienced carpenter."

Marc glanced darkly at Naomi who was standing several feet from him. She had the nerve to smile back at him and wave. After the accident, Marc hadn't wanted to be in charge of anything. His confidence had taken a hit. Now he just wanted to be one of the volunteers. "I've helped my grandfather and dad complete additions to my parents' house," Marc admitted with frank reluctance, "and I've built a few garages with friends. But I'm not an expert. Someone else—"

"We don't need experts," Ms. Washburn interrupted in her usual brisk tone. "Today we are going to finish setting the trusses to support the roof and start laying the roof boards. I want you to direct the actual building from now on. And since you're not working, I hope you'll ramrod Jeannie's house, too."

Marc hesitated. It was a lot of responsibility. Was he ready to shoulder that much? He'd slept better the past two nights with Amigo snuggled beside him. Almost five hours a night. Still, his usual confidence hadn't yet returned. "Maybe some other guy here knows more."

"No, I've talked to them all and you seem to have the most experience. So you're it." She gestured for him to go to the front of the men and women who'd gathered to work today.

Marc did not want to put himself forward. However, he heard in the woman's tone, no quarter was to be given. And Rosa was looking at him, and so was this new woman, Jeannie. *Suck it up, Chambers. And get going.*

Drawing up the reserves of his tattered self-assurance, he began explaining and directing the crew.

Everyone listened with a respectful silence and started working. The welcome sound of hammering and talking took off, a blessed distraction.

Marc was kept busy, answering questions, demonstrating how and where to drive in nails. However, he could not stop keeping track of both Rosa and Johnny. It was as if he had some kind of radar on them.

Consuela was knitting under the oak tree once again. Johnny was busy practicing pounding nails in the nearby stump. On the outside of the house's shell, Rosa was helping to nail sheeting over the bare frame walls. Then with several other volunteers, he hefted one side of the first truss and raised it into place.

The triangular trusses rose, one by one, and were nailed into place. When all the trusses were secured, creating the triangle of the future roof, impromptu shouts of victory broke out. Marc added one of his own. He turned to find that Rosa had appeared at his elbow. Her pretty face radiated joy. Again, his hand rose to touch her cheek, to connect with her bright warm luster. *No.* He raised his arm and swiped the perspiration with his sleeve, hoping no one had noticed or guessed his original intent.

* * *

A horn honked. Rosa along with everyone else turned to the source of the sound. A white panel van that had a dark pink logo of two bright pink cupcakes and "Sweets Two Go" painted on its side had just pulled up.

Very aware of Marc so near and the fact that she thought he had been reaching for her cheek, Rosa welcomed the interruption. For that one brief moment as the final wall truss rose, she had felt completely connected to Marc. They had shared a moment of pure joy. She scolded herself for this lapse in keeping her distance from Marc. She turned and moved away toward the van.

Two women of the same height with short curly red hair and similar features—who looked like identical twins—bustled out. Wearing crisp blue jeans and white smocks dotted with tiny pink cupcakes, they swung open the van's rear doors. Soon they hustled past Rosa and started setting up a table under a tree near the street. Hammering slowed and then stopped altogether.

Eleanor Washburn hurried around Rosa to the women. "May I help you?"

"Hi, we're your caterers today—Sweets Two Go. And yes, we're twin sisters. Everyone asks," one of the women said, motioning toward the van and then her twin. "We're sorry we're late. We were supposed to be here earlier but we had a flat tire on our way. We have your coffee and doughnuts."

"There must be a mistake," Ms. Washburn said. "We didn't order any—"

The other twin interrupted her while unrolling white paper over a table and taping it down. "We know that, but we don't know who paid for it, either."

"What?" Ms. Washburn said.

Johnny took Rosa's hand. She glanced down. Her son

was holding her hand but looking back at Marc a few paces behind her. The expression on her son's face told her everything about what her little boy thought of Marc Chambers. His face bore all the signs of hero worship. Her jaw tightened. *I didn't want this to happen, Lord. When the house is built and Marc disappears from his life, I don't want Johnny hurt.*

The nearby conversation between Eleanor and the caterers continued. "We just got a printed note with what the person wanted to be delivered and a hundred-dollar bill," the same twin said.

"In the mail with a local postmark," the other added with a nod. "We're a reputable company."

"That's right," her twin agreed as she and her sister hurried back to the van. "We couldn't keep the money if we didn't fulfill the order." The two returned, bearing two large cellophane-covered boxes of doughnuts.

Then from the van, they carried two large barrel-shaped red-and-white drink dispensers, one marked "Coffee," the other "Hot Water." Within minutes the refreshments were all laid out on the long table.

Rosa hadn't been hungry till the scent of sugar doughnuts came to her on the breeze. Eleanor Washburn stood nearby, frowning at the tables. The twin caterers turned expectantly toward her. "Okay, we're ready!"

Rosa glanced behind her. She wasn't the only one who'd smelled the seductive doughnut scent. Johnny was already tugging her hand toward the tables. From the corner of her eye, she saw that Eleanor Washburn was probably thinking what she was thinking. Doughnuts were made for eating; doughnuts couldn't be ignored.

A sideways glance showed Rosa that Marc looked puzzled. Was that an act? This was something a good man like he might do. Was this another gesture of this man's kindness?

Eleanor waved her hand high. "We'll take a ten-minute break! Come and get it!"

Dropping her hand, Johnny ran fast and was the first one to the table. "Do you got ones with red jelly in them?" he asked.

His voice was loud enough that everyone heard him. A chorus of friendly chuckling added zest to the midmorning treat. Rosa suddenly experienced the true meaning of this Habitat for Humanity project. It was about giving and loving, two very good things in this often sad world.

Rosa tried to ignore the fact that as they all went forward toward the refreshment table, Marc had moved closer to her. He hung back while she went ahead to supervise her son.

"Hey," Johnny said, turning back to Marc, "I got you the best one." Running over, he offered Marc a plump white powdered-sugared Bismarck.

Rosa watched Marc hesitate as he looked down into Johnny's hope-filled, eager face. Just as Rosa was about to intervene and distract her son, Marc reached over, touched a finger to the white powdered sugar and then pressed it to the tip of Johnny's nose. Johnny beamed at this bit of friendly teasing. "Thanks, Johnny. It looks like it is the best one. Are you sure you don't want it?"

"No," Johnny said as he handed it to Marc, "it's for you."

At that moment, Rosa knew trying to keep Johnny and Marc apart might already be a lost cause. But a boy needed a man in his life and Trent was not ever going to fill that role. He'd started a new life in Florida.

Behind her, Eleanor mused aloud, "Who would send us a hundred dollars worth of doughnuts and coffee?"

"We don't know," the twins said in unison, "but here's your change." They handed Eleanor a white envelope.

Rosa bit into a sugar-coated cruller and rolled the sweetness around her mouth. Johnny was taking Marc over to see his progress at nailing into the stump. Rosa followed them, letting herself for once enjoy the sight of her son happy in the presence of a kind man. Yet Marc Chambers was complicating her life.

That followed because Marc Chambers was complicated, a complex man. Gray smudges still underlined his solemn eyes. And the accident in January no doubt still weighed on him.

Would he end up hurting her son even unintentionally? She hoped not, but she couldn't think of any way to stop what was happening. Perhaps she should learn more about Marc. *I hate prying into other people's business.* Her own experience as an unmarried pregnant teen, an object of gossip, had given her a healthy respect for the privacy of others.

Naomi appeared at Rosa's elbow. "Your son is good for Marc. I was afraid…" Naomi pursed her lips for a moment. "Anyway I think everything is going to work out now."

Rosa nearly turned to Naomi to ask more about what she meant. Then her son shocked Rosa by asking, "Mr. Chambers, will you come to church with us this Sunday?"

She stared at Johnny in disbelief. Where had this come from?

"That's right," her grandmother, Consuela, said, "I told Johnny he should ask you. I think you would like our church, Senor Chambers. We got good singing."

Rosa now stared at her grandmother, astonishment vibrating through her.

"Well, I'll give it some thought, Johnny," Marc said. "I usually go to church with my grandmother."

"She could come, too!" Consuela invited.

Rosa could understand her son's motives, but her grandmother had never played matchmaker before. She gave her grandmother a look that said, No, *Abuela,* no, don't try to bring us together.

Marc walked reluctantly down the center aisle at the venerable Hope Community Church, Johnny tugging him along. In front of them, the two grandmothers, Naomi and Consuela, were chatting quietly as they went down the aisle. Rosa moved silently beside Marc. She certainly wasn't making it easy for him to resist the pull toward her.

He tried to keep his eyes from shifting to her. But he had never seen her in a dress before, and the flattering royal blue summer dress that she was wearing attracted him magnetically.

Consuela led Naomi into a row halfway down the aisle. Rosa followed them. Marc tried to let Johnny go in after his mom to be a buffer between Rosa and him. But the child shook his head and pulled back. Marc didn't want to make a fuss so he sat down next to Rosa. Johnny climbed happily into the pew on Marc's other side. A shiver climbed up and down Marc's neck as if everyone around was looking at him.

The pianist began playing a lively hymn and Marc rested his aching back against the pew. Lifting trusses had stressed his muscles that hadn't done heavy work since January. A song leader motioned for them to stand and Marc rose with everyone else. Rosa offered to share her hymnal with him. He sang along with her to "Tis So Sweet to Trust in Jesus."

The song was one he'd sung since he was a child, but now Rosa's sweet soprano voice joined his. A wealth of feeling, more than he thought possible, flowed through him with the melody. He clamped down on his slipping composure, hiding his reaction. But the music and Rosa's voice had uncapped a deep well of feeling and healing within him. Then out of the blue, he thought of Caroline Mason, gone now. He mourned her once more. His chest tightened, hurting him. *This is hard, Lord, so hard.*

Johnny reached up and slipped his hands around Marc's bent elbow and leaned his head against it. The simple gesture of affection released Marc's lungs and he was able to breathe easily again. Then Rosa glanced up at him and smiled. Her smile warmed him within like afternoon sunshine.

The hymn ended and with much rustling, everyone sat down. The pastor spoke a prayer. Then there was more singing. Marc settled into the service. It was different and yet the same as the small country chapel he had attended since birth. Being in a new church helped him experience worship as if it were all new to him. His lungs expanded and his back rested more comfortably against the pew.

Finally, the pastor began his sermon by quoting verses from Matthew. "'Come to Me, all you who are weary and burdened, and I will give you rest. Take My yoke upon you and learn from Me, for I am gentle and humble in heart, and you will find rest for your souls. For My yoke is easy and My burden is light.'"

Marc squirmed. The verses didn't ring true to him. How could a burden be light? This year he'd struggled to carry a load beyond any he'd known before. He suffered it then—a virtual weight bearing down on his lungs and heart. *Lord, how do I take up Your yoke and learn how to find rest?*

Caught in his own tangle of pain and loss, he found suddenly that Rosa was urging him up for the closing hymn. He must have completely zoned out through the whole sermon.

That shook him. Gaps in his short-term memory had been common for a couple of months after the accident.

With relief when the last note was sang, he made his way toward the church doors. He would go home and busy himself with yard work and homework. And the cloud from January would lift again—for a while. If he hadn't accepted Johnny's invitation, he'd have gone to the chapel as usual. And this crevice in his armor wouldn't have opened up and let the pain leak in again.

He would just stop saying yes to everything Johnny asked. *I can't be more than a friend to him. And right now I can't be a very good one.*

Outside under the tall oaks, pines and maples surrounding the brick church, Marc looked toward his truck, the way home where he could be by himself with just Amigo for company.

"Senor Marc, why don't you come home with us for lunch?" Consuela invited with a smile. "I made my own *abuela*'s recipe for tamales, wrapped in fresh corn husks."

"Yes!" Johnny agreed loudly, pumping his arm.

Marc started to say no and was cut off by his grandmother's faster than the speed of light acceptance.

Rosa drew in a sharp breath. *No, Abuela, no.* Sitting beside Marc in church and managing to appear nonchalant and indifferent to him had been a test. She'd tried to concentrate on the worship service. But being so close to a good man who didn't want to become involved with her, whom she couldn't involve in her life, had become a torment. One so slow and painful it had seemed like a twisted wire dragged through her by a turtle.

Anyone with one half an eye or ear could see that Marc was still suffering. Marc had his problems and she had hers. And her responsibilities. Johnny always came first no matter what.

"We'll just follow you home," Naomi said, taking Marc's arm.

"*Bueno,*" Consuela replied with a cheery grin, taking Johnny's hand and leading them toward their car.

Rosa avoided Marc's eyes and started off toward her blue beater. Once inside with her grandmother and son, Rosa started the car. As she backed out, she said stiff as starch, "Please don't do that again without consulting me. I have a lot of homework to do today before I go to work tonight at the Truck Stop."

"Rosalinda, we all have to eat," Consuela said with a teasing lilt in her tone.

Rosa glared at the windshield and turned onto the street, heading home. She glanced in her rearview mirror and glimpsed Marc's red pickup. She fumed over her grandmother's blatant matchmaking. *When we are alone tonight,* Abuela, *we are going to have a long talk.*

But first she had to get through lunch with Marc. And think of some way to safeguard Johnny from Marc. Marc wasn't the kind who would hurt a child. But when their house was finished, Marc would slip out of her son's life. And leave Johnny heartbroken. Why didn't her grandmother get this?

Chapter Five

As Rosa ate the tamale lunch, she now understood something of how a person in a straitjacket must feel. Marc sitting beside her, she'd nearly pinned her arms to her sides to avoid bumping or touching him. With his elbows also tight against his sides, Marc obviously grappled with the same constraint in her tiny apartment.

Yes, her grandmother and Naomi had engineered the seating arrangement so that Marc and Rosa sat side by side at their short narrow table. As usual, his nearness made breathing normally difficult for Rosa.

She fired a pointed look at her grandmother. *Your matchmaking hasn't gone unnoticed,* Abuela.

Consuela just smiled as she stepped to the nearby sink.

"Those were delicious," Naomi said, rising to help Consuela clear the table. "I'd never had homemade tamales."

"I love *abuela*'s tamales!" Johnny piped up.

"I must agree," Marc said. He glanced at his wristwatch, no doubt anxious to leave.

Rosa didn't blame him. She was weary from hours of trying not to show any reaction to Marc's presence. Right now she wanted only to rest her head in her hands. Her one hope, the hope that was dwindling moment by moment, was that he and Naomi would leave before Trent's weekly call came.

Earlier at church, Rosa had not failed to notice all the silent speculation about Marc and her. Inquiries about her "new" friend would crop up. Would anyone believe her that Marc was really *Johnny's* friend?

Now that the meal had ended, Marc made as if to rise.

And was forestalled. "You cannot leave without dessert," Consuela said, opening the freezer and taking out a tub of rainbow sherbet. "We always have sherbet after a good spicy meal."

"Sherbet," Johnny repeated with approval.

Rosa's eyes went to the clock. Trent's call would come soon. The thought chafed her. Why didn't her grandmother understand that she didn't want Marc to be here when the weekly call came?

Consuela dipped into the tub of sherbet, loading bowls with it. Naomi began passing them around the table.

Rosa forced a smile. "I guess I have time for dessert. But then I'm afraid I'll have to excuse myself. I have studying to do."

"Me, too," Marc echoed. "But, Consuela, this has been a great meal."

"Mr. Chambers, do you like soccer?" Johnny asked, spooning up a heaping teaspoon of the red raspberry stripe of sherbet.

Rosa tried to think why Johnny would ask this.

"I don't know much about it, Johnny. I played football in high school."

"You'd like soccer," Johnny was saying. "It's a neat game. The coach called and said he was going to start a team for both boys and girls. The first practice is this week. Will you come?"

Why hadn't she heard about this before now? Rosa's spoon stopped in midair. "*Abuela,* I didn't know anything about this soccer team."

Her grandmother shrugged.

"I want you to come, too, Mama," Johnny assured her. "But I know that Mr. Chambers will like it. A lot."

"Johnny, Mr. Chambers is a busy man," Rosa intervened.

"I know but—"

The minute hand moved one more notch, bringing the dreaded call closer still. Her neck tightened. "Johnny," she said sharper than she meant to, "don't pester Mr. Chambers."

Her son's face fell and he put down his sherbet spoon. Then the phone shrilled. The weekly call had come. Johnny turned to the phone but didn't move.

Rosa wished she knew whether these phone calls were good for her son or not. They never failed to prick her tender spot, caused by Trent's betrayal. Her head began to pound. The phone continued ringing. Each one increased the pressure in her head. "Answer it, Johnny."

With obvious reluctance, he got up and went to the phone on the kitchen wall and pulled the receiver down. The three adults listened as Johnny replied with a variety of unenthusiastic "yes, sir," "uh-huh," and "no, sir."

Marc looked to her, asking her silently who had called Johnny.

She couldn't bring herself to name who'd called. She rubbed her taut, painful forehead. Johnny hung up and came to the table. "That was my dad, Trent," Johnny told Marc. "He calls me every Sunday."

"Maybe he could come to your soccer practice," Marc suggested.

Rosa realized she was clenching her teeth. Trent had

spent only an hour with Johnny the last time he'd visited his parents here. Bitterness like acid sluiced through her.

"He can't come. He lives in Florida with his wife. That's too far to come here much." Johnny stirred his sherbet, apparently no longer hungry. "He says I'm going to have a baby brother or sister next year."

This announcement slammed into Rosa like a clenched fist. Not because she still had feelings for Johnny's father. But because Trent and his wife were certain to be anticipating this baby. Something he had never felt for Johnny. Johnny had been an inconvenience, an embarrassment. And this new child would get Trent's attention as her son never had. A monthly check and a weekly phone call did not a father make.

I did this to my son. The chain of guilt slipped around her neck, tightened, choking her. *Father, help my son.*

"I'll come to your soccer practice, Johnny," Marc said. "But just once."

Her son's face glowed with pleasure.

Still struggling to show no reaction to the new baby announcement, she grappled with this new dilemma— soccer, Johnny and Marc.

Her head throbbing now, Rosa wished then that Marc Chambers weren't so good to others. *That's stupid,* she told herself. He'd proved over and over that he was a man with a kind heart. Perhaps it wouldn't be a mistake to let Johnny form a friendship with this man. But what if Marc fell in love with someone and started a family? Like Johnny's natural father had?

At the thought of Marc falling in love and marrying some faceless, nameless woman, Rosa put down her spoon. The January accident may have sidelined Marc for most of the year. But it wouldn't be long before pretty coeds would start pursuing Marc. She watched her rainbow sherbet melt.

Marc's future wife wouldn't want him hanging around with another woman's son. And Rosa couldn't blame her.

A week later, outside his grandmother's white frame house, Marc gripped the bottom of the new window he and Luke were installing. Opposite Mark and inside, Luke braced one hand at the top of the window and one near the sill below.

The whole farmhouse and yard were being spruced up for his grandmother's eightieth birthday celebration on Labor Day. Marc tried to concentrate on the physical task at hand. However, Luke's preoccupied expression kept intruding.

Marc knew his brother well enough to know that Luke was chewing on something. Was he just mooning over Jill? She was a nice enough girl but... Rosa's face came to mind. And there was no comparison. Jill was just a girl. Rosa was a woman, a beautiful, caring woman.

Marc's jaw tightened. He had enjoyed Rosa's company too much that night at the bowling alley. And afterward that moment in the rain when he had nearly kissed her had come back to mind way too often.

A cicada screeched nearby, startling Marc out of his reverie. "Get the shims, Luke," he said. As the mail car stopped at the box on the road, the three dogs as usual began barking at it. Amigo had joined Gram's two golden retrievers who had readily accepted him as a new pal.

Marc watched Luke hold the level to the window frame to check it before they secured it in place. If Luke needed another favor—if he needed another date, then Marc would say no and stick to it.

At Luke's word, Marc pulled the caulking gun off his tool belt and ran a line of caulk around the seam between the window and the house. After some more quick work, they'd firmly fixed the replacement window in place so the house was ready for the storms of winter.

Luke came out the back door and approached Marc. "I want you and Rosa to go on another date with Jill and me," Luke finally blurted out.

"No, Luke." Marc walked away from his brother toward the remaining three windows they were putting in today.

"Marc, hear me out."

Marc propped his hands on his belt. "Luke, why? Didn't we Chambers pass muster the last time?"

"Sure we did. Jill's dad is cool with us spending time together now."

"Then what's the problem?" Marc asked, not keeping the irritation out of his tone.

"I'd just feel better about it. I mean, it's so much easier if you and Rosa are along." His brother ran out of words and stood facing him with a pleading look.

"Let's start the next window," Marc said.

Evidently willing to let Marc have time to ponder, Luke helped Marc take the wrapping, the shipping straps and the bubble wrap off the next new window. When the window was in, Luke sent Marc the question with his expression.

"No," Marc said, "I can't ask Rosa for another favor."

"Why not?"

I nearly kissed Rosa—that's why. His pulse sped up at the memory and this sharpened his tone. "Just no." *I can't let that happen again.*

Luke looked like he wanted to argue, then he just shrugged. The two of them worked in silence then. Marc wondered if he were being a jerk for not helping his brother. But someone had to put a stop to this recurring drift where he always ended up being in Rosa's company.

Rosa Santos was a wonderful woman but whenever he

thought of dating Rosa or anyone, his stomach clenched so tightly he couldn't eat.

He knew this came from losing Caroline in the accident. Who could have predicted she would be driving home to Madison that awful day, caught in the same chain reaction? Her death had been a cruel twist. Didn't people understand what this accident had cost him? His physical wounds had healed, but not his head. Or was it his heart? How long would it take to feel normal again? Would he ever?

Marc pulled up to the new soccer field at the edge of town. He'd hoped for a thin attendance but now he parked in the midst of a crowd of vehicles. Their little town of Hope, though growing, still behaved essentially as a small town. Coming to watch Johnny's soccer practice would open him and Rosa for speculation and gossip. How could he prevent that?

I should have just said no. But so far he hadn't been able to do that to Johnny Santos. The dejected look this boy had worn after speaking to his natural father had haunted Marc.

Marc opened his truck door.

Johnny, dressed in white shorts and T-shirt with blue vertical stripes greeted him there, "Hey, Mr. Chambers! Hi!"

Marc grinned at the boy. "Hey, neat uniform."

Johnny radiated pleasure. "It's cool, isn't it? Mom bought it."

"Your mom takes good care of you."

"Yeah." Johnny grabbed Marc's hand. "Come on. You can watch from over here with my mom."

Marc let Johnny drag him over to the bleachers set up on the sidelines where parents, primarily mothers, congregated. Rosa occupied the near end of one bleacher. Not faraway, Consuela sat beside his grandmother, both ladies comfortable in lawn chairs.

Marc lifted a hand in greeting to them all. Why hadn't his grandmother told him she was coming, too? *We could have driven together.* And then he could have made it seem more like he'd just come as a friend of the family. Was that why Naomi hadn't let him know? Was she matchmaking?

"*Hola!*" the knitting grandmothers called and waved in unison.

Uncertain, he waved back as he mounted the bleachers. With every moment his misgivings deepened. He was fairly sure that the two grandmothers had plotted together about the Sunday tamale lunch. What else did they have up their matchmaking sleeves?

As Marc approached Rosa in the bleachers, she gave him a smile he believed was forced. "I hope this isn't cutting into your study time, Marc."

Marc grinned back in kind. "I was getting tired of studying. Needed some fresh air." He sat down near her, yet on a different level bleacher. He wanted to be friendly but didn't want to give the wrong impression to the watching mothers, many he recognized. He and Rosa were not a couple and he didn't want to start gossip.

"I don't know much about soccer," Rosa said.

"Me neither," he confessed.

"But Johnny is excited about it." She shrugged as if to say, "So I am, too."

The evening sun had lowered but still radiated summer-like warmth. He tried to relax, tried to tell himself just to enjoy the experience.

"Hey! Is that you, Chambers?"

Marc turned toward a deep voice that sounded familiar. He recognized an old high school friend. He rose, his hand outstretched. "Spence! What are you doing here?"

The blond athletic man scaled the bleachers. "I'm the coach." Spence shook his hand. "See, those are my girls." He motioned toward two little blond girls who were kicking a black-and-white ball back and forth between them.

"I noticed this is a coed team," Marc commented. *Spence has daughters?*

"Yeah, at this age boys and girls can compete together. Which kid is yours?" Spence turned sideways to view the children on the green.

"I don't have any," Marc admitted reluctantly, aware of how many ears must be taking this all in. "I'm here to watch Johnny Santos." He turned and motioned toward Rosa. "This is his mother Rosa, a friend of mine."

"A friend?" Spence grinned knowingly. "You always did know how to pick out the prettiest girls."

Marc didn't know what to say. If he said that Rosa wasn't his romantic interest, that might insult her. He struggled to think of something tactful to say.

Rosa spoke up. "Marc is helping to build my house over on New Friends Street."

"Is that the Habitat house?" Spence asked.

"Yes, the first one," Rosa replied. "There will be three. I'm on the corner lot."

Spence nodded and then excused himself. "Gotta go. Time to start. Nice meeting you, Ms. Santos. Great seeing you again, Marc."

Marc waved and then sat down again. He couldn't help looking back at Rosa. But she had turned her gaze on Johnny. Marc followed suit. Spence lined the children up to practice dribbling. Marc watched each child try to move the ball back and forth, keeping it between their feet. The balls went every which way. And with their attention fixed on their own ball, the kids began colliding with each other. These mishaps gave Marc a few grins.

"It's kind of like watching a human pinball game," Rosa commented in an undertone.

Marc laughed out loud and then tried to disguise it as a cough. He watched Johnny working his ball, his whole concentration on the ball. To Marc, it looked as if Johnny definitely played better than the other kids. "He might be good at this," Marc murmured for Rosa's ears only.

"I hope so. He really wants to play."

One of Spence's girls ran over to the sidelines and handed something to a woman dressed in designer jeans who must be her mother. Spence had been two years ahead of him in school.

Spence was still ahead of Marc in life. Spence had a wife and two daughters old enough to play soccer. Envy stung Marc. He tried to oust it and failed. Except for some savings in the bank and a retirement fund, what did Marc have to show for the decade since high school?

He looked at Rosa out of the corner of his eye. And then forced himself to face forward. He found it harder and harder to resist staring at Rosa. For some reason, she could gain his attention by doing absolutely nothing but being near. And each time he studied her, he found something new and appealing. Now he was noticing her sandaled feet—so dainty, so feminine. He jerked his attention back to the practice.

When it ended, Johnny ran over to Marc, panting with exertion and probably excitement. "Did you see me kick the ball into the goal?"

Marc rose and ruffled Johnny's bangs. "I sure did. I think you're going to be a great soccer player. But you've got to stick to it."

Johnny nodded vigorously, making his bangs flop up and down. The sight tugged at Marc's sense of humor.

Before he thought it through, he said, "You need a haircut, Johnny."

"*Si,*" Consuela agreed, appearing with Naomi at her elbow. "I will sit him down and trim it before Senora Naomi's big party."

"I've just invited Consuela and her family to come to my big birthday party this weekend," Naomi said with an impish grin.

Marc stared at her. The artery at his right temple began to throb. So far, he'd put off having words with his grandmother about this overt matchmaking. Now however, he should speak up—even if he had to disclose his new round of nightmares to show her why she shouldn't be trying to encourage a romance between Rosa and him. However, the thought of revealing this pressed heavily onto his lungs. *No, I can't. I don't want to cause everyone worry all over again.*

Spence came over. "Great to see you, Marc. Johnny is very enthusiastic." Then Spence looked from Marc to Rosa with evident speculation. "I hope you'll come and watch him again, Marc."

Marc's tongue was tied. *How do I get out of this? There has to be a way that won't hurt Johnny.*

Between classes, Rosa sat in the campus library on the mezzanine overlooking the main floor where the circulation and reference desks were. She had come to read her composition textbook. Also while trying to come up with a topic for an essay, she fretted over Marc attending her son's soccer practice.

She tried to shut out the clear-cut memory of Marc's enthusiastic encouragement of her son. Johnny had blazed with sunny smiles all the way home, telling and retelling what he'd done at practice. He'd been glad he'd been able to kick a goal while Mr. Chambers had been watching. She might as well try to hold back the morning sun as try to blot Marc Chambers out of her son's life.

Instead of silence, the library hummed pleasantly with low voices. Then she heard a very familiar voice and looked down. Marc stood at the reference desk.

For once, she had the opportunity to study him without his knowing and away from matchmaking grandmothers and her son. She let her eyes roam over his broad shoulders. His shoulders carried heavy burdens both physical and emotional and bore them without complaining. The overhead lights glinted on the reddish highlights in his short-cropped hair. Clean-cut described Marc to a tee.

She sighed without making a sound. She had been trying to come up with a polite way to decline Naomi's birthday party invitation. Without luck.

Marc moved away and sat down at a table below. Rosa forced herself back to reading the textbook open in front of her. She began to jot down a few notes on her steno pad. But her traitorous eyes kept straying to Marc. A trace of another feeling, a romantic feeling tried to stir. She pushed it down without mercy.

Still, this romantic stirring triggered the inevitable fear, fear which washed through her like a cold rinse. Would the sting from Trent's rejection of her and their son ever heal?

She began to write furiously, forcing herself to think of the assignment. Then somehow interrupted or alerted, Rosa glanced downward. She saw the young red-haired girl, Penny Mason, whom Rosa had twice before seen watching Marc on campus. Penny had stopped just inside the library doors and gazed at Marc's back.

Rosa had connected Penny with her sister, Caroline, and Caroline's death with the January accident and with Marc who had been involved in it. She couldn't regard Penny's standing and watching Marc with a lack of concern. Rosa tensed. Was Penny one of those people who would express anger at Marc because he had survived while her sister had died? Was Penny going to say something to Marc? Would it be something kind or something unkind? Would that matter to Marc? Either might be hurtful to him.

So far Penny had not approached Marc. Rosa didn't think Marc had glimpsed Penny. That eased Rosa's mind and she glanced down at her text. But she couldn't stop herself from watching them from the corner of her eye.

Then upsetting Rosa, Penny walked directly to Marc and sat down across from him at the table. She put her backpack down and leaned toward Marc, obviously speaking to him.

Rosa sat forward and watched, unable to look away. She wished she could hear what Penny was saying to Marc. How would it affect him? *It's none of my business.* But Marc had become important to her.

Marc and Penny continued talking. Rosa noted the rigidity in Marc's posture, a stiffness that had not been there before Penny sat down. Even though Rosa couldn't hear a word, she felt as if she were eavesdropping. Still she couldn't look away.

Penny finished talking, nodded once and then opened her book and began reading. Marc went back to reading or looking like he was reading. Rosa watched, thinking that she must be overreacting. She hoped that Penny taking the initiative to speak to Marc would turn out for the good.

A few minutes passed and then she looked back down again. From the corner of her eye, she glimpsed Marc rise, gather his materials and leave.

Rosa tried to start reading her textbook again. But soon the insistent prompting to go after Marc became undeniable.

Sometimes God had nudged her to show His love and care to another person. Whenever she had ignored promptings like this, she had always regretted it.

With a grimace at herself, she pulled her materials together and headed down the steps and out of the library. When she stepped out into the early September afternoon, she realized that she didn't have a clue of which way Marc had gone.

She looked around the parking lot. She spotted Marc's truck far to her left. She walked toward it, wondering what she should say if Marc were in his truck. As she approached, she saw him sitting behind the wheel. His expression was pained. That cut her deeply, moved her forward. She reached the pickup. Without asking for permission, she opened the passenger door and climbed in.

Marc turned to look at her. His eyes appeared filled with misery and looked moist.

Her hesitance to intrude evaporated. "Marc, what is it? Penny?"

"How did you know?" His voice came out like a croak.

She sat sideways toward him. "I put it together a few weeks ago. I saw Penny watching us in the library and remembered who she was and…about her sister Caroline."

He hung his wrists on top of his steering wheel and bowed his head between them. "You know about Caroline, about her dying in the accident?" he asked, his voice muffled.

"Yes." Saying the single syllable shook her. "It was a dreadful accident. Dreadful." She saw just one tear fall to Marc's lap. She turned away to look forward. No man liked to be seen wrestling with such sorrow.

And most men didn't know that talking things out

helped. She forged ahead for the sake of this good man. "Were you good friends?"

He didn't answer right away. Finally he muttered, "She was my first girlfriend in high school. That didn't last but our friendship did."

"It's hard to lose a friend." Rosa clenched her hands into fists to keep from reaching for Marc.

"I can't get over her dying that day. I was so close but I didn't, couldn't know she was. I keep thinking there was something I could have done, should have done."

"Survivor's guilt," Rosa murmured, her heart breaking for him.

He drew in air. "The mist just came up—it swallowed us and formed a sheet of ice under our wheels. I lost control... cars were spinning, sliding..." He shuddered.

"It's more than that," he said, still hanging his head. "Caroline was about to be married." He spoke as if each word was a heavy weight. "To a great guy in Madison."

"Oh, Marc." She couldn't help herself. She gripped his shoulder. "Oh, Marc." She couldn't think of another word to say. She'd carried heavy sorrow like this. She bowed her head and began praying for this good man, for Caroline's fiancé and family, for all those who had lost friends in the January accident.

Marc looked at Rosa out of the corner of his eye. What would she say if he confessed, "My rig was the first to skid?" From her bowed head, he knew that she was praying. That struck him. How many times had he prayed for relief from the pain, the sadness, the guilt? With no result?

Her dark chocolate hair had fallen forward, hiding her face from him. His fingers tingled with the temptation to sift through it. She'd dressed in red as usual and wore the turquoise-and-silver necklace, too. The cool silver tempted his fingertips there, so close under her chin. He gripped the steering wheel.

His mind dragged him back to Penny and their brief conversation about Caroline. It had sliced open his guilt, his sorrow like a razor blade. *If only I'd left the night before as planned, I wouldn't have been there.*

But in January, Naomi had fallen and sprained her ankle. The rest of his family had been down with the flu. So he'd had to stay home until Naomi could get around by herself. Just before dawn that dreadful day, she had shown him she could get around with the walker. He'd left right after that and driven into the mist of freezing rain…

The loud bell inside the building sounded the change of classes. Rosa raised her head. "I have to go to class."

"Me, too," he managed to say, though his emotions lay open, raw and stinging.

They both got out of his truck. They walked side by side toward the nearest building. He wanted to say something but couldn't think of anything that sounded right. Inside, Rosa turned to walk away.

"Thanks," he murmured.

She merely smiled and waved. Then she walked away. He couldn't help himself. He watched her go till she moved out of sight. Other students passed by him, laughing and chatting. He stood like a rock. Yet inside him an earthquake raged.

The physical consequences of the January accident came alive with pain. His bones that had been broken and the muscles that had been torn now smarted and then burned like fire, as if they were reminding him, prompting him to suffer all over again. What if he never was able to put this out of his mind? What if Caroline's death and his guilt was going to tear him apart like this for the rest of his days?

If I hadn't been there repeated in his mind for the

millionth time. Nothing would have changed except he wouldn't have been a part of the suffering and sorrow. And that sounded harsh, selfish even. Why should he have gotten off scot-free when Caroline and others hadn't?

On the balmy and sunny afternoon of Labor Day, the day of his grandmother's eightieth birthday party turkey roast, Marc wasn't in the mood to celebrate. Trying to decide how to handle his attraction to Rosa and Johnny's need for a man in his life had kept him up last night. Still trying to hide his sleeplessness, he followed Naomi out of the kitchen.

He carried her new sunflower-covered picnic tablecloth. While he hurried to shake and lay it over the long rectangular table that his grandfather had built, he tried to decide how to handle today. How could he keep his mom especially from jumping to conclusions about Rosa and Johnny's presence here today? The day loomed like a mine field. His grandmother and Rosa's grandmother were the wild cards. Who knew what they had planned to bring Rosa and him closer today?

Marc turned to find Rosa, Consuela and Johnny coming toward Naomi. His whole body contracted with tension. Rosa didn't help matters by looking pretty in a new red blouse and jeans. Beside her, Consuela and Johnny were smiling. Though evidently trying to hide it, Rosa appeared stressed.

His mind flashed back to those moments shared in the cab of his pickup. He couldn't recall exactly all that he'd said to her that day. That worried him. He walked toward her.

Johnny raced to meet Marc. "Where's your dog? Mom says you have a dog now."

As if on cue, Amigo propped his front paws on the

chain-link fence of the dog run and began barking. Marc grinned. "There he is." He pointed to the dog run. "Go introduce yourself. His name is Amigo. Your mom named him that."

"Wow!" Johnny raced to the dog run where Roxie and Dottie had joined in welcoming Johnny. Ready to play.

Marc greeted a beaming Consuela. Rosa looked up at Marc. "What can I do to help?"

He stared down into her face; the smooth olive skin drew him. He imagined cupping her soft cheek with his palm. "Help?" he repeated, lost in her dark brown eyes. The sound of the barking receded in his mind. Words he knew were for Rosa simmered just inside his lips, pushing him to say all he was feeling for, for sweet, loving Rosa.

Chapter Six

Rosa gazed up into Marc's open honest face. The pull to move closer to him strained, conquered her better sense. Resistless, she leaned forward.

A familiar voice intruded. It broke the invisible connection. "Hey, Rosa! Hi!" Luke loped toward her.

"Luke," she gasped. She nearly blurted out, "How are you and Jill doing?" But she caught herself just in time. "Great to see you again."

"Ditto. Hear you were the one who helped Marc here get his own pet." Luke nodded toward the dog run. Johnny had already entered it and begun petting the three delighted dogs, who were leaping and licking Johnny's delighted face.

She shrugged. "What can I say? I'm a soft touch." She noticed Luke looked different today. The confident and expectant expression he wore contrasted so from the insecure one he'd worn throughout their double date. Did this mean anything, anything *she* needed to know?

"Rosa—" Naomi appeared between Marc and Luke "—so glad you have come." Then Consuela joined them. Naomi swept Rosa and her grandmother up into the festivities and made them known to arriving guests. The turkey being roasted on the rotisserie grill scented the air, making Rosa's mouth water.

Shaking hands and smiling, Rosa couldn't help beginning to relax and enjoy herself. She had come out of friendship for Naomi. She had come on her guard and for good reason. When Marc had greeted her, what she feared had almost happened. He had looked at her that way, that way that singled her out as special. She found it harder and harder to keep up a barrier against him.

Today everywhere she looked Johnny hovered right beside Marc. And she couldn't muster the energy to try to draw Johnny away from Marc. Seeing her son so happy soothed her soul. Yet honest worry wouldn't release her.

And Luke's bright expression never wavered. What did he have up his short sleeve? And would it involve her or Marc?

The Chambers family members—aunts, uncles, cousins—and longtime neighbors gathered and filled the yard. Among the crowd, Rosa noticed a few people obviously tracking the interaction between her, Johnny and Marc. These people wore speculative expressions.

However, again Rosa couldn't summon any sense of caution. She sat sipping homemade lemonade under a large shady oak, happy to let the cheerful chatter carry her along on its easy current. Luke greeted people and laughed a lot. Rosa caught Marc staring at his brother. Was it because this was unusual behavior for Luke?

Then a middle-aged couple, a slender blond woman and a stocky man with crew-cut gray hair, appeared from the lane between corn rows. They entered the yard bearing wrapped gifts. Rosa watched them approach. They must be the next door neighbors.

Just then she realized what this meant. She recalled that the mailbox next door read Bud Tracy Luke Chambers.

These were Marc's parents. The thought shocked her like an electrical short.

Naomi brought them directly over to her. "Tracy, I don't think you've met the Santos family. Rosa, this is my son, Bud, and his wife, Tracy, Marc and Luke's mom and dad. And Tracy, beside Rosa is Consuela, Rosa's grandma, and over there—" Naomi pointed "—that's Johnny, Rosa's son."

Rosa stood and offered her hand. "Hello." She didn't trust herself to say more. Why hadn't she thought about the probability of Marc's parents attending this event? Was Marc's mother already "eyeing" her? Or was it her imagination?

Tracy looked past Rosa, evidently also quick to observe Marc on the other side of the yard. He was pushing Johnny on the tire swing on a tree. "Luke mentioned your son a few days ago," Tracy said, turning back to Rosa.

"Really?" Rosa replied, but did not trust her voice to ask for more.

"Yes, Luke said that you had gone to high school together—" Tracy's blue eyes that were so like Marc's studied her "—and that you were going to the local college now."

"That's true." Rosa hoped someone would come and distract Tracy Chambers. Now Rosa recalled *why* Luke hadn't wanted his parents to know about his dating Jill. Tracy Chambers must be one of those women who eagerly anticipated weddings and in quick order, grandchildren.

Not a bad attitude in general, Rosa thought. Yet Johnny's birth grandparents lived less than a half hour from where Rosa stood this minute. And they wanted nothing to do with Johnny. Another poisoned thorn, still buried deep inside Rosa's heart.

No doubt the new grandchild in Florida would be welcomed. Rosa fought the stinging bitterness, which tried to ooze up and spoil this pleasant day.

After exchanging a few more comments with Rosa, Tracy and Bud soon had to move away to speak to other friends. Tracy, however, did glance back at Rosa several times. Fretting, Rosa sat down and tried to reclaim her earlier tranquil mood without much success.

The turkey was carved and served along with a myriad of side dishes. Rosa had never tasted turkey cooked like this. The flavor was amazing. Finally, everyone gathered around the picnic table, dominated by Naomi's cake, a vast lavishly decorated chocolate sheet cake, sporting two candles, one the number eight and the other a zero.

"Cool candles," Johnny said. "Eight-zero, eighty, cool."

Nearby Consuela chatted with a couple of Marc's great aunts. But Rosa kept a watchful eye on her son from the end of the table. He, along with every other child, hovered around the cake. In fact, youngsters ringed the table, not wanting to miss any of the cake festivity.

Rosa smiled, reading Johnny's expression and posture. The cake tempted him to steal a finger full of chocolate icing. Rosa was about to say something when Marc pulled Johnny back a few inches to stand in front of him, planting one hand on each of his shoulders. Her son grinned up at Marc. This simple gesture spoke volumes of volumes. Rosa loved it and feared it.

Marc's mother, Tracy, who also appeared not to have missed this telling piece of body language, lit the candles and clapped her hands. "Okay, let's sing to the birthday girl!"

The singing, the blowing out the candles—Naomi asked the children to help her—and the cutting of the first slice kept everyone busy. And then Luke called out, "Jill!" He went jogging down the drive toward Jill and her father.

Everyone turned to watch a thrilled Luke walk up the drive with Jill beside him. In silent communication, Rosa and Marc's eyes met across the table. Then watching Luke present Jill to Naomi, Rosa wondered at Luke's choice of this time and place to let it be known that he'd begun dating Jill. It certainly showed courage.

"I didn't know Luke had this much guts," Marc murmured in her right ear, matching her sentiment.

She gave a start and glanced up. She'd been so busy watching Luke that she hadn't even noticed Marc moving near her. The nape of her neck tingled at his nearness. She nodded. "What happened, do you think?"

"I guess he decided to get it over with in one big bang," Marc said.

Luke reached the others grouped around the table. "This is my *girlfriend,* Jill, and her dad, Tom Bellers, from Rhinelander." After this blanket announcement, Luke took Jill to his parents. Rosa caught the emphasis on the word *girlfriend.* The simple pride of the word radiated from Luke, unseen but palpable. Rosa warmed herself in Luke's innocent triumph.

The exciting announcement over, the two women, who were helping with the cake, snapped back to doing their jobs. One sliced cake into generous squares and the other scooped up mounds of vanilla ice cream. Then though every eye might have politely turned away from ogling the newcomers, Rosa reckoned every ear remained tuned into what Luke was saying to and about Jill. Most everyone here had probably watched Luke grow up. Their happiness at his bringing a girl home to meet his family spread out through the smiling guests eating cake and ice cream, chatting and watching the children take turns on the tire swing.

Sudden and unexpected, Rosa's throat thickened with emotion. Luke's obvious pride in presenting Jill to his family and friends affected her with a force she'd never have predicted. It left her feeling discarded, abandoned, unvalued.

"Su tiempo vendrá." The soft words took Rosa by surprise. She turned to find her grandmother standing on her other side. Her grandmother had just told her, "Your time will come."

"Si, Abuela," Rosa whispered back—without any real conviction that her time for this kind of joy would come. She had made a wrong choice and it had left her life and Johnny's forever changed. Rosa forced a smile. Marc remained near her and that gesture of understanding made her lonely reality harder to take. But she wouldn't let selfishness spoil Naomi, Luke and Jill's special occasion.

Jill waved to Rosa who waved back and also winked. Jill giggled at this. Rosa was happy, sincerely happy for Jill, a sweet girl who'd found a good man who loved her. And Rosa was glad for her, wistfully glad. *Be happy, Jill. Be very happy.*

At only 9:37 a.m., Rosa wanted to spit nails hard and fast. She bent forward and tapped her forehead onto the steering wheel center. Why couldn't anything ever be simple? This trip today was packed with such importance to her grandmother. *And me.*

"The car? It won't go?" her grandmother asked from beside her.

Rosa let her forehead rest against the wheel. "The car. It won't go, yes."

Silence. A charged one. Then Rosa heard her grandmother weeping quietly. The sound magnified within her head. *Abuela* never cried.

Rosa raised her head. "Don't worry. I will call for help."

"But everyone is working." Consuela dabbed at her eyes. "Or too busy."

Rosa didn't even stop to think further. She pulled the phone book from under her seat, where she kept it for emergencies like this, looked up a name and punched it into her cell phone.

When Marc answered her call, she said quick and urgent, "Marc, I need your help. My car has died on County K and I'm driving my grandmother to see my grandfather at the VA, the veteran's administration hospital. Will you please come and help us?"

"Where on K?"

"Near Pine Lake School."

"I'll leave now."

"Thank you." She tried to put all the gratitude she felt into her voice. She closed her phone, got out and paced beside her car, watching. Her nerves revved like a motor on high idle.

Within ten minutes, Marc turned onto County K. He parked in front of the car. "What's wrong?"

Tears sprang to her eyes and she turned away.

He stood there, waiting. "Do you need a jump?"

"I need a better car." Facing him, she tried to smile and shrug it off. "Today is my grandfather's birthday. He has Alzheimer's. I'm taking my grandmother to see him at the VA hospital in Madison. That's why I called. We have to get there and be back in time to meet Johnny's school bus." She drew in air to keep from crying.

"Let me take a look. It might be something simple that I can fix. I always carry my tools in my truck."

She popped the hood and he leaned over it. Within a few minutes, he shook his head. "It's beyond my mechanic abilities." He turned to her. "Do you have roadside service with any company?"

"No." Rosa folded her arms and looked down, defeated.

He slammed the hood shut, pulled out his cell phone and hit the button for his roadside service. "Where do you want it towed?"

Rosa told him the name of the garage near her apartment. Then they waited by her car. Rosa rubbed her arms, chafing over the delay, over her grandmother's crushing disappointment and her own. *I want to see my abuelo.* Then the wrecker appeared in record time. The man offered to take Rosa and her grandmother home.

"No, they need to go to the VA," Marc said. "I'll take them." The wrecker drove away.

Rosa knew she shouldn't accept Marc's gracious offer but Consuela was already limping toward Marc's pickup. And refusing Marc's help was not an option, not today. Gratitude washed through her, carrying her forward in its momentum.

Beside the pickup, Rosa stood back, attempting to let Consuela get in first. However, Consuela insisted on watching how Rosa got in using the handhold. With a little help from Rosa and Marc, Consuela managed to land on the high seat beside Rosa. Soon Marc, Rosa and Consuela sat in a row, heading for the interstate. Rosa made certain to keep a few inches from him, her awareness of him so heightened.

"We are very grateful," Consuela said. "This is my husband, Juan's, birthday and I have made him his favorite cookies." Consuela lifted the wrapped box on her lap. "My poor Juan has the Alzheimer's."

"I'm sorry to hear that," Marc said.

And being Marc, he of course sounded genuinely

sympathetic. Rosa fought the urge to slip her hand into the fold of his elbow. As she sat so close to him in his cab, memories of that double date returned. "How's the Jill and Luke romance going over with your family?"

Marc glanced at her. "My mom's already knitting baby clothes."

Rosa laughed out loud.

"You joke, Marc," Consuela scolded with a smile. "But women love babies. And *abuelos* do, too."

"*Abuelos?*" Marc asked.

"Grandfathers," Rosa replied.

"*Si*, my Juan adored Johnny," Consuela said. "This illness is hard. It robs a family."

Each word her grandmother said jabbed Rosa like a needle. Johnny had been named for her grandfather Juan who had been the provider and backbone of their small family. Her grandfather had taught her about growing things, the work he loved above all other, and he'd taught her about faithfulness, kindness and about so much more.

"From what I hear, it's an awful disease." Marc merged onto the interstate which would take them south toward the VA hospital.

Rosa blinked away the moisture that had come to her eyes. Thanks to Marc they would be with her *abuelo* today. "I wish we could visit him more often," she murmured.

"God knows we do our best," Consuela said, patting Rosa's arm. "But thank you, Senor Marc. I did not want to miss my Juan's birthday."

"No problem. Glad to do it."

Rosa noticed Marc needed a haircut. His hair waved up along his neckline, tempting her to smooth it down. Rosa folded her hands in her lap and gazed at the mixture of forest and farm land that they were driving through. Marc was the kind of man who made a woman want to depend on him. *I can't give in to that temptation. Marc carries enough already.*

Marc pulled into the parking lot at the VA hospital in Madison. Merely looking at the hospital sent a shudder of dread through him. He hadn't been near a hospital since his long stay in January. Consuela's handicapped tag made it possible for him to park close to the entrance. Resisting his rising dread at having to enter a hospital again, he helped Consuela down. Before he could offer Rosa his hand, she had scooted down to the asphalt on her own. He felt cheated.

He admitted to himself that he had wanted to touch Rosa's hand and wanted to help her. He'd already known that she carried a lot of responsibility but he hadn't known that she had a grandfather with Alzheimer's. In spite of the sick ache at the bottom of his stomach, he took a deep breath, preparing to enter the hospital.

"You don't need to come," Rosa said, giving him a hesitant look.

"I'll come in." He offered Consuela his arm. *I'm not a coward.*

The older woman smiled and took his arm. *"Gracias."*

"My pleasure." Marc led Rosa and her grandmother inside and then he let Rosa lead them.

As he expected, walking into a hospital rocked his senses. The disinfectant smells unleashed a torrent of sensations and memories of his accident and long days and nights hooked to machines that shushed and beeped. He'd had broken ribs and right arm, a collapsed lung and lacerations on every piece of exposed skin. Pain—so much pain, and he'd been helpless.

He focused on taking one step and then the next. *They need me. Keep it together.* They walked down a bright corridor, the Alzheimer's wing. Marc held tight to his cascading reactions. Rosa and Consuela needed his support.

Consuela saw her husband. In spite of her limp that looked painful, she hurried ahead to the small man in a wheelchair sitting in the solarium near a window. Marc fell back and let Rosa hurry forward. Both women spoke a flurry of rapid Spanish.

Marc moved around them, standing a short distance away. His breathing had become shallow and the cold sweat continued. He watched the man look at Consuela and his granddaughter without recognition. Consuela soldiered bravely on, speaking to him, stroking his face.

To keep busy, Marc brought a chair for Consuela to sit on. She lowered herself and holding the man's hand, caressed it with such love that Marc had to turn away.

He busied himself bringing another chair, one for Rosa, from the opposite side of the room. When he had seated Rosa, he stood back alongside the window. Still breathing shallowly, he prayed for strength.

Consuela opened the box she had brought for her husband and waved a white-powdered cookie under his nose. Suddenly he smiled and said, "Consuela."

Rosa's grandmother began to weep, but her smile never wavered.

Marc watched Rosa help her grandmother feed her grandfather bites of the cookie. The older man appeared frailer than Marc had expected, but perhaps this came from this terrible disease. As he watched the three, his own unnerving reactions waned. His breathing eased.

Marc surprised himself by speaking up. "It's such a nice day. Would they let us take Juan for a walk on the grounds?"

The nurse that had been hovering nearby came right over. "Yes, of course. You can take him out the door at the end of the room and into the courtyard. We try to get our patients outside in the sun as often as we can."

Consuela popped up. "*Bueno*. My Juan always loved being out under the sun." Rosa replied with only a thankful glance for Marc.

His heart rate accelerated again. Marc took charge of the wheelchair and headed for the door to the courtyard. After walking Juan around the courtyard twice, Marc sensed that Consuela needed to rest again. So he led them to a park bench. Rosa and Consuela sat down and continued carrying on a conversation without any help from the man. They also kept feeding him bites of cookie. Marc leaned against a nearby column, still slightly unsteady.

"Johnny," said the older man and then he looked at Rosa. "Johnny."

Marc's chest tightened. This sudden recognition seemed a gift straight from God. Consuela cried out with the joy of it.

Tears falling, Rosa kissed her grandfather's cheek. "Johnny is fine. *Johnny está bien*. He loves you. *Johnny te ama*." She swallowed down her tears. "I love you. *Te amo*."

"*Te amo, mi marido,* my husband," Consuela echoed and kissed her husband's gnarled hand. She pressed it to her tear-dampened cheek.

Marc had to turn away. The expression in Rosa's eyes could have made a stone weep. *I want to make things easier for this family, this woman, but how?* Why did life have to be so harsh? And what could he do for Rosa?

He pulled up in front of Rosa's apartment with just minutes to spare. While Consuela, who insisted she didn't need any help, hobbled inside to lie down, Rosa and Marc strolled toward the bus stop where Johnny would soon arrive. Exhausted, Marc had spent all his energy enduring the stress of a hospital visit.

"Thank you so much for taking us," Rosa said. "I wouldn't have called you—"

"I'm glad you did," Marc interrupted.

She glanced up at him. "I knew that most everybody else would be at work. I hoped you didn't have class. We didn't have time to make it there and back before Johnny came home—"

"I'm glad I was available. I haven't taken a formal job. I just help my dad and Luke with the farm." He didn't want her thanks. He had done so little.

The yellow school bus rolled toward them and stopped, some metal creaking and gears grinding. Johnny ran down the steps straight into Marc. "Mr. Chambers, hi!"

The joyful greeting moved Marc. He swept the boy up into his arms and then back down. "Hey, Johnny!"

"What are you doing here?" Johnny asked, walking alongside Marc and grinning ear to ear.

Before he replied, Marc caught Rosa's unspoken admonition. *She doesn't want him to know where we've been. Why?* "Your mom had some car trouble and I drove her home."

Johnny didn't miss a beat. "Okay. Will you come to my first soccer game, Mr. Chambers? It's this Thursday at six o'clock."

"Sure," Marc said, looking into Rosa's eyes, ignoring his failed intention to keep his distance. Johnny was a great kid and Marc realized for the first time how much he cared for the little guy. The trip to the VA had opened him to the need to show what he honestly felt for Johnny. That couldn't be wrong. *I can do this. I'm getting better. And I want to go to Johnny's game.* "Sure."

The day of Johnny's first soccer match, Marc parked his truck in the gravel lot along the soccer field. More parents had come out for the first game of the season than the first practice. He hoped the game would be a good one for Johnny's sake. Scanning the bleachers, he had no trouble picking out Rosa with her blue-and-red plaid blouse and dark hair and olive skin. She stood out like an exotic tree amid a pine forest. He ignored the inner voice, telling him not to sit near Rosa.

He knew the moment she saw him. Her face lifted in a smile and her hand rose. Spirits soaring, he climbed up the bleachers two at a time and sat down beside her. "Hi," he said, unable to say more. Her joyful expression at seeing him lifted him, filled him to the brim. He had to fight the urge to reach for her hand.

"Hi," she said back, still beaming at him.

"Car?" he asked.

"Fixed," she said.

Fortunately the game started then, saving them from this monosyllable conversation. Marc watched the game, picking up the rules as he observed the play. As Rosa had so aptly described it, the first game of the two coed soccer teams was like a grand human pinball machine game. However, Marc noticed that whenever Johnny got the ball, he had better control of it. Twice he managed to get the ball close to the goal.

"He's a natural," Marc murmured.

"Really?" Rosa replied quietly. "I'm not just imagining it because he's my son?"

Nodding, he kept his gaze trained on the other players who were running, tripping, bumping into each other, but mainly on Johnny. During a break in play, a mom came by with an empty plastic gallon ice cream container which bore the inscription Team Donations Please.

Marc dug into his back pocket.

Rosa gripped his wrist. "No, Marc, you don't have to—"

"Oh, let the man give," the woman said.

Marc recognized her then. She was the wife of the coach and his old teammate, Spence. He grinned. "I want to, Rosa." He pulled out a bill and dropped it in the plastic bucket.

It pained him to watch Rosa pull out two singles and drop them in.

I wish I could help her more.

Then she yawned and tried to hide it. She noticed him watching her and smiled. "I had to work the night shift last night."

"Do you have to work nights often?"

"No, I was covering for a friend who just had outpatient surgery. She'll be fine in a week."

Marc wracked his brain, trying to think of a way to be of help to Rosa. This woman carried the burden of a son, an aging grandmother and a grandfather in a nursing home. She worked as a waitress and on her Habitat house and took classes and studied. Compared to her, he led a carefree life. *I want to help her, Lord,* he repeated silently.

In spite of all the fumbling and tripping during the match, the parents cheered on their children, calling out their names. Rosa and Marc did the same, shouting encouragement to Johnny. And to their delight, Johnny ended the game by making the winning goal.

Marc jumped to his feet, applauding and shouting. Rosa turned to him. He threw his arms around her and they did an impromptu victory dance and shout. Several people patted Rosa and him on the back, congratulating them on Johnny's goal.

In passing, one man said to Marc, "Your boy has real talent."

"He does, doesn't he?" Marc replied, not correcting the man. *My boy.*

And then Johnny was running up the bleachers to them. "Did you see me? Did you see me make that goal?"

Marc swept Johnny up into his arms. "Did I see you? You bet I did! You were great!"

Rosa took Johnny's face in both her hands and turned his face back and forth. "You were wonderful! *Maravilloso!*"

Marc put Johnny back on his feet but kept the boy's hand. The three of them began walking down the bleachers together. Marc's chest expanded with exhilaration. "I think that this boy deserves an A & W root beer float, don't you think, Rosa?"

She hesitated a moment and then with a glance at her son's hopeful face, she replied, "Yes, a black cow float would be a good celebration."

Rosa, Marc and Johnny reached the bottom of the bleachers and were greeted by an exultant Consuela and Naomi. "And we'll join you at A & W!" Naomi exclaimed.

Suddenly Spence appeared at Marc's side. "Sorry to interrupt. But Marc, I just found out that I am going to have to travel for work next month. I was wondering if you could come to the practices before and then take over for the few games I'm going to miss."

Marc's breath caught in his throat. Two answers flew to mind—yes and no!

Rosa's breath caught in her throat. *No, this is too much to ask.*

"Sure," Marc said. "I'd enjoy it."

Rosa's breath rushed out. "Are you sure—"

Johnny's shout of jubilation swallowed up her words of caution. Then others were coming up to congratulate them on Johnny's winning goal. The Chambers and the Santos families moved with the crowd toward the parking lot.

"Can I ride with you in your truck?" Johnny asked Marc.

Marc looked to Rosa and so did Johnny. How could she say no to them? "See you two guys at A & W."

The A & W had drawn quite a crowd so the five of them sat outside on one of the picnic tables. As Rosa watched Marc and Johnny discussing the game as if it had been a World Cup match, she reveled in the moment. She sipped the sweet creamy black cow and stirred the pale brown froth with her straw.

People glanced their way and many waved. She waved back, letting herself enjoy being here with Marc and her happy son. A memory she would cherish. Though the fear of Johnny becoming too attached to Marc still lingered, it had ebbed to a distant foreboding.

If Marc said he would help with Johnny's team, he would. Marc was too good a man to promise what he couldn't deliver. He wouldn't abandon Johnny. *I knew that before tonight.* And his agreeing to stand in for the coach had somehow drained power from her insecurity.

Now that they were well into September, dusk came a bit earlier. As the shadows lengthened, Consuela with Johnny and Naomi walked toward their respective cars not far away. Rosa found herself walking Marc to his pickup. Too late, she realized that the two grandmothers had somehow maneuvered her into walking him to his truck. She sighed inwardly. They were conspiring to matchmake again. But she didn't care. Tonight all worries had taken flight, vanished.

The two of them halted by his driver's side door. An invisible, cozy warmth enveloped her. "Thanks for the root beer floats," she said, gazing at him in the low light.

"My pleasure." He lowered his face toward hers.

He's going to kiss me. The realization sent tremors of expectation through her. Not one warning bell clanged.

He bent lower still and brushed her lips with his. Rosa couldn't think; she could only feel, experience the wonder of Marc Chambers's velvet touch.

"I've wanted to do that for the longest time," he whispered.

She couldn't form words so she smiled and leaned forward. He bent his face. With the barest movement she brushed her lips across his. Just as he had done to hers.

He pressed his palm against her cheek and stroked his thumb across her cheekbone once, twice. She closed her eyes, the better to savor his touch. Then he kissed her forehead, sparking more wonder. "Good night, Rosa."

"Good night, Marc." Such simple words said but packed with such meaning. She forced herself to step away.

Without another word, he got into his truck. She watched him drive away. Then she walked the short distance to her car. Did her feet touch the earth?

Slipping behind her wheel, she did not meet her grandmother's eyes, face reality. She wouldn't let anything dissipate her gladness at this moment. *Tonight I will be happy. I will not worry about tomorrow.*

She drew a ragged breath and started driving toward home. Her heart sang an old Broadway musical song, "I Feel Pretty"—and she wanted to dance, clap her hands and tell the world. *Nothing bad is going to happen. Not this time. Please, Lord.*

Chapter Seven

~⌒~

His neck muscles tight, Marc stood beside his friend Spence. They watched the soccer team gather on the field. Marc churned with second thoughts about this coaching. Overnight a prelude of the winter to come had blown south from Canada and was scheduled to blow on eastward tomorrow. Now, however, the sun hid behind the chilling gray veil of layered clouds. The young soccer players all wore sweaters as did Marc and Spence.

"Don't look so tense," Spence said. "With kids this little, you can't do much wrong as a coach. I just use what I learned from my, from our, years of being coached." He gave an apologetic smile. "A little toned down. We aren't coaching a team playing for a state championship."

Marc nodded with understanding. Yes, their coaches in high school had driven them to give their best and they had. This gave Marc something of a wake-up thought. Over the past months, Marc hadn't let his mind go back to high school *at all*.

Throughout those years Caroline had been a girlfriend and then a friend. And he had not wanted to think of her young and alive because then memories of the accident fatal to her tagged along. As a consequence, good memories of those times had been sacrificed. *That isn't right. I should remember both good and bad times.*

"Just watch me coach and you'll be fine." Then Spence clapped his hands and shouted, "Let's get started! Gather 'round, team!"

Unable to stop himself, Marc glanced this way and that, seeking Rosa. He glimpsed Naomi and Consuela. The two grandmothers were bundled up in their lawn chairs on the sideline, knitting. And then his gaze found Rosa. She sat hunched forward on a bleacher, wearing a red-and-white University of Wisconsin sweatshirt with the hood pulled up. Her hands were pressed between her knees for warmth. Where had all their summer days gone?

He waved; she waved back. Even from here, he caught the brightness of the smile on her pretty face. His mouth curved up in response.

Spence started the kids running around the field for team exercise and waved Marc to join him and the kids. "Let's get our exercise, too," Spence teased.

Marc loped along at the easy pace. Johnny slowed up and jogged alongside Marc. And then Rosa appeared at Marc's elbow. "I needed to get my blood pumping, too," she explained.

Marc adjusted his stride to keep them in step.

"How's Amigo?" Johnny asked, breathing hard.

Marc grinned. "Amigo is just fine. Let's concentrate on soccer, okay?"

Johnny grinned. "I can run faster than you can!"

"Bet?" Marc asked, speeding up. Rosa laughed out loud and raced to keep up with them.

Rosa waved to them as they passed her.

At the end of the run, Marc panted. His muscles had warmed and his face was flushed. These pleasant sensations gave him confidence. And Rosa touched his shoulder and whispered in his ear, "Thanks for doing this. Thanks." Then she jogged back to the bleachers, leaving him warmed heart-deep.

The practice flew past, fast and energetic. At the end, he hurried to greet a smiling Rosa coming down the bleachers.

A yelp of pain and a sudden outcry turned Marc away.

He saw Consuela lying on the ground and his grandmother kneeling beside her.

"Abuela!" Rosa cried out and began running toward her grandmother.

Marc with Johnny also raced toward Consuela and reached her first. "What happened, Gram?"

"She stood up and then just collapsed," Naomi replied.

Rosa knelt beside Marc. *"Abuela,* what's wrong?"

Consuela groaned. She rubbed her side. *"Mi ca…dera duele."*

"It's her hip," Rosa said.

"Yo no me puedo levanter." Consuela panted with the exertion of speaking.

"She can't get up." Rosa looked to him.

He read her request for aid clearly. "Spence! Help me carry this lady into the backseat of my grandmother's station wagon. We've got to get her to the hospital. Now."

Marc and Spence picked Consuela up, making her cry out sharply again. Carrying her as gently and quickly as possible, they laid her on the long wide backseat of the station wagon. Naomi got behind her steering wheel. "I'll head right for the hospital E.R. She's not having a heart attack or a stroke. She's not bleeding, so don't worry."

Marc slammed the door by Consuela's feet. And his grandmother started the car and drove away. He turned to Rosa. Her anguished expression wrung his heart. He gripped her hands in his. "I'll meet you at the emergency room. Are you okay to drive?"

She squeezed his hands in reply and then released them, taking Johnny's hand and running toward her car. Marc jumped into his pickup and waited to see if her car would start. It did. He gunned his pickup out onto the county road with Rosa's sedan right behind him. He began praying, "God, let Consuela get help, the right help, right away."

He chanted this prayer over the ten-mile ride to the hospital. Then he parked in the E.R. lot and hurried to the entrance to stand beside Rosa and Johnny. Two nurses, one male and one female, were helping Consuela out of his grandmother's station wagon and into a wheelchair. Marc put his arm around Rosa's shoulders. She looked up into his eyes.

He pulled her closer. "Don't worry." He said the words but wished he could *do* something for this brave woman. *Lord, help us out here, okay?*

Consuela's face twisted with pain. The sight pierced Rosa's heart and she gasped at the phantom pain. Marc's arm around Rosa's shoulders gave her the extra stamina she needed to remain calm, at least on the outside. Johnny would be quick to pick up her alarm. *I mustn't frighten him.* Staying close to Marc, she gripped his hand and began a soft flow of reassuring words in Spanish—for Johnny, for Consuela—for herself.

Naomi came to stand on her other side, taking Johnny's free hand. Their presence held great comfort. Rosa walked through the automatic doors. Recalling Marc's distress at the VA, she glanced up, but read only concern in his eyes.

Consuela was rolled into an examining area. Rosa squeezed Marc's hand, asking him without words to care for Johnny. He nodded. She bent to her son's level and cupped his soft cheek in her palm. "Johnny, please stay here with Marc and Senora Chambers."

Her son nodded, his bangs flopping up and down. The sight caught around her heart. Consuela hadn't felt strong enough to stand to make the effort to cut his hair. *I should have insisted she go to the doctor. I knew she was walking with more and more difficulty.*

Naomi put a hand on Rosa's shoulder. "Now don't you go worrying. We'll take care of Johnny. You go with your grandmother." Naomi patted her. "Go on. He'll be fine."

Rosa nodded her agreement and momentarily pressed her hand over Naomi's.

Then she hurried into the examining area where they'd taken her grandmother. One last glance backward showed her Marc and Naomi, each holding one of her son's hands and walking toward the line of chairs in the waiting room.

The loss of Marc's nearness left her bereft. Marc glanced at her over his shoulder. His gaze connected with hers, sending her reassurance without words. She felt it, a ripple of warmth through her. How she longed to ask Marc to come with her, but that wasn't possible. Instead, she faced what she must. *Lord, help.*

Hours passed as the initial exam, the taking of X-rays and now the consultation took place. Consuela had been given a shot for the pain and was resting on a gurney in the hallway near radiology. Johnny, Naomi and Marc had come to hear the prognosis with Rosa. The hours in the hospital had sapped her hope, made her feel remote as if Marc's earlier comforting touch had not been real. She stood apart with her hands tucked under her arms. She kept her eyes from seeking Marc. Was it because she was so close to tears?

A doctor motioned them into a small room where he clipped the X-ray onto a glass panel. "I'm afraid your grandmother isn't going home tonight."

"What is it? Did she break her hip?" Rosa asked, unable to keep from shuddering with dread.

"No, I really don't know how she has been managing to walk at all," he said in a matter of fact tone. "The ball of her hip is nearly eaten away because of bone on bone friction. The cartilage in her right hip is completely gone and must have been for a long time." He shook his head. "She needs a hip replacement ASAP."

"A hip replacement?" Consuela said in a weak voice. "Oh, no."

Rosa gripped her hand. "Don't worry. *No te molestes, Abuela.*"

Marc came up behind Rosa and rested a hand on her shoulder.

"Yes, fortunately," the doctor went on, "we've had a cancellation in surgery tomorrow afternoon. I'm going to schedule your grandmother with our orthopedic surgeon. You are in good luck twice because he is going on vacation in three days."

Surgery? Tomorrow? Rosa was a ship in a storm at sea, tossed on wave after wave. She caressed her grandmother's hand, trying to grasp this development. Marc gripped her shoulder. Johnny came to Marc and took his free hand. Rosa wanted to turn and bury herself against Marc's reassuringly solid chest.

On Consuela's other side Naomi approached the gurney. "Now don't you get upset, Consuela. The surgery isn't fun, but you'll be able to walk normally again very soon."

Naomi looked to Rosa. "And don't you worry about Johnny. You need to stay here with your grandmother."

Rosa had already thought of this problem. She couldn't leave her grandmother here alone. The thought hurt Rosa's heart. She wiped away a stray tear. "Yes, when she's upset she speaks in Spanish. I—"

"Don't worry," Marc said.

"We understand perfectly." Naomi patted Consuela's hand. "Rosa, give us the key to your apartment. Marc can take Johnny home to get his nightclothes and stuff for school tomorrow. I'll come back in the morning with a change of clothing for you. And I'll sit with you through the surgery."

"No, you don't—"

"No argument," Marc said.

"Someday you may have to sit with Marc while I have something fixed." Naomi grinned.

Rosa smiled at Naomi's comment. "Thank you."

"*Gracias,*" Consuela agreed. "*Gracias a Dios.*"

"We're glad to help," Marc said.

Rosa bent. "You mind Mr. Chambers and Senora Naomi, okay?"

Johnny nodded with a solemnity that nearly broke her heart. "*Abuela* is going to be okay?" he asked.

Consuela spoke up, "I will be fine, Johnny. Don't worry."

Rosa kissed his forehead and rose. The nurse had come to show them to the elevator and to Consuela's room. Rosa gazed into Marc's caring blue eyes and whispered just for him, "I'll be all right." He nodded and she handed him the spare house key, their hands brushing.

Again she wished she could ask him to stay longer. Instead she rushed to catch up with the gurney. As she stepped into the elevator, she waved to Johnny. Leaving him was hard but he would be safe with the Chamberses, with Marc. Marc raised his hand in farewell to her. It enfolded her as a gentle prayer. *Gracias a Dios por Marc.*

Feeling flattened by all that had just happened, Marc let Johnny out of his truck. On the way home from the hospital, he had decided that Johnny should stay with him. He didn't want Naomi to have her sleep interrupted.

Marc hoped and prayed that he wouldn't wake Johnny with any of his nightmares. He hadn't had one for about a week. But a visit to the E.R. and all this trouble might trigger another onslaught. *Lord, I can't have a nightmare tonight. And please comfort Rosa.*

To say that Johnny was not himself appeared to be an understatement. The normal happy kid had been replaced by a somber, sad-eyed little boy. As they walked toward the house, Amigo, Roxie and Dottie began barking. Dropping his backpack, Johnny let go of Marc's hand and raced toward the dog run.

Marc picked up the dropped backpack, followed, watching the boy enter the dog run and throw his arms around Amigo's furry neck. The other two dogs woofed and licked his face. Marc smiled, his load of worry lightened by this genuine welcome. Dog therapy—there wasn't anything like it.

Johnny looked to Marc. "Can Amigo come in?"

"Sure." Marc heard a car and turned.

Naomi drove into the garage and came out. She clapped her hands. "Roxie! Dottie!" Her golden retrievers bounded out of the dog run and straight to Naomi.

Amigo, however, stayed beside Johnny. Marc waited till his grandmother reached them.

Naomi said, "You boys go up and get Johnny settled

then come down. I have supper in the Crock-Pot. Sloppy Joes."

Not for the first time, Marc thanked God for this indomitable woman. Rosa had this kind of strength, too.

"I love Sloppy Joes," Johnny said, brightening.

"Great. See you soon." Naomi walked toward the back door with her dogs, frisking behind her. Marc offered his hand to Johnny who took it. Amigo loped along beside them and then led them up the stairs. Inside the apartment, Johnny halted, looking around, appearing deflated. Marc put a hand on his shoulder. Johnny turned into Marc, wrapping his arms around Marc's waist and burying his face in Marc's shirt.

Marc felt the telltale tremors of crying. *Poor kid.* He put his hand on the top of Johnny's head as if blessing him. "You're going to be okay. And so is your grandmother."

Johnny looked up, tears on his cheeks. "But my other grandmother Maria went to the hospital and never came home. We put flowers on her grave sometimes."

This jogged Marc's memory. Jill had said that she'd lost her mother and Rosa had said she'd lost hers, too. Maria, Rosa's mom. "Johnny, Consuela will come home." Marc hoped he was telling the truth. Things could happen during an operation, bad things. *God, be with Rosa.*

In the dimly lit room, Rosa curled up in the recliner beside her grandmother's bed, keeping vigil. Her back muscles had twisted into a spring about to break. The large round clock on the wall ticked past the minutes. 11:37 p.m. The white curtain between the two beds in the room had been pulled so that Rosa couldn't see into the hall. Her grandmother's roommate, fast asleep, made a kind of whiffling sound. In the hush of night Rosa counted the beats of her heart.

This was a painfully familiar setting. Dark memories flocked around her like ugly black bats, wings flapping. Her mother had been in this hospital many times over the course of her fight against ovarian cancer. Rosa scrubbed her taut face with her hands as if she could rub off the insistent fear. She must not let worry overwhelm her.

This is my grandmother, not my mother. This is just an operation to fix a hip. It's not life-threatening. I must have faith. I must pray. But she found she couldn't pray. Her mind shuddered with panic, leaving her thoughts incoherent.

The new nurse walked into the room. "Hi," the woman said softly.

Rosa sat up, watchful and glad of any company. "Hi."

The nurse wrote her name, "Kathy," on the white board at the end of the bed. And then proceeded to check Consuela's vital signs. Rosa watched, glad of the distraction and comforted by the nurse's competent manner.

"Do you need anything?" the nurse asked Rosa.

Rosa thought of the list of things she needed, primarily an infusion of peace. "No, I'm fine," Rosa mouthed the polite phrase.

"Let me know if you or your grandmother needs anything. If you're hungry or thirsty come to the desk, okay?"

Rosa smiled, grateful for the woman's kindness. "I will."

The nurse left them then.

Consuela shifted on her side toward Rosa. "I can hear you thinking. Hear you worrying all the way over here."

Rosa got up and went to hold her grandmother's arthritic hand. "Sorry. It's just... I should have made you go to the doctor."

"This is not your fault. This is just old age. Now go back

to that chair, cover up and get some sleep. Worry never changes anything, *querida*."

Worry never changes anything. Rosa obeyed her grandmother at least on the surface. Soon she was reclining under a cotton blanket and trying to appear to sleep for her grandmother's sake. She closed her eyes. *Abuela* had it right. Life came with no guarantees. Anything could happen but why in Rosa's case was it always something bad?

The next morning, Marc entered the surgical waiting room, hoping to be of some support to Rosa. The TV was playing CNN quietly. He scanned the crowded room for his grandmother and Rosa. Naomi waved and Rosa looked up. He moved to her side, reaching for her hand. "How are you?"

She took his hand. "I'm fine," Rosa replied with the polite answer. She appeared to study his face. "Did Johnny get off to school okay?"

Marc slipped into the open seat beside Rosa, reluctantly releasing her soft hand. "Yes, I dropped him off on time and then I had a class. But I don't have anything for a couple of hours. Any word about your grandmother?"

"She is doing well." Rosa wrapped her hands around each other and lowered her chin. Her hair fell forward, veiling her face.

Marc yearned to smooth her hair back, keep their connection.

"She should be out soon," Naomi added. She rose. "Now that Marc is here I'm going to take a short walk. I need to keep moving or my joints freeze up on me. Whoever said getting old isn't for sissies knew what he was talking about." Naomi grinned and walked out of the waiting area.

Rosa looked into his eyes. "I'm so grateful for all your help—"

He interrupted her. "You'd do the same for us." Then he couldn't say more. She was so beautiful even in this setting, so vulnerable.

"I've called my church and they've added me to the meals for the sick program to start when my grandmother comes home. Some of the waitresses I work with are covering my hours at the truck stop. And if I need someone to watch Johnny, I have names to call so you don't need to keep—"

He raised a hand, interrupting her. "Johnny is fine with me." He made his tone emphatic. "I think it's best if he stays with me till you are able to handle him and your grandmother. Amigo is making this easier on him." He coaxed her with his gaze.

Rosa nodded, worrying her lower lip.

A stranger who looked like a staff member walked into the room. "Rosa Santos?" she read from a clipboard.

Rosa raised her hand and stood up. The woman approached them and sat down in the seat beside Rosa that Naomi had vacated. "Hello, I'm your grandmother's occupational therapist. I need to discuss arrangements for her after she is released in a few days."

"A few days?" Rosa repeated, sounding worried as she sat again.

Marc tensed. *So soon?*

"Yes," the woman explained as if she'd heard this objection all too often, "we usually only keep our hip replacement patients long enough to help them recover after the surgery and to teach them the skills they'll need at home."

"What skills?" Rosa looked worried now.

"Your grandmother will be using a walker for a few months and then a cane. You need to check to see if your doorways are wide enough to accommodate her walker. If not, she may have to go to a nursing home till she is well enough to use a cane."

Rosa looked even more worried.

Marc touched her arm, his mind racing to find a way to help.

"Is that going to be a problem?" the occupational therapist asked.

Rosa's shoulders sagged. "Yes."

Marc put an arm around her shoulders. "Don't worry. We'll figure this out." Rosa gave him a feeble smile. And he gave her shoulders a reassuring squeeze. *Whatever it takes, Rosa.*

Five days later, Naomi drove up to her back door. Marc was waiting there. Rosa got out and opened the car door to the backseat.

"*Abuela,* here we are." Rosa was happy yet uncertain, happy that her grandmother was doing well enough to leave the hospital, but uncertain about this arrangement. It seemed as if she were accepting too much from the Chambers family. Wrestling with this debt, Rosa unfolded the walker, clicked the latches and placed it in front of her grandmother.

"Now don't feel as if you're imposing," Naomi said, joining Rosa. "I wouldn't have invited Consuela if I didn't want her."

Consuela gripped the walker with both hands and rose to her feet. "We are grateful, Naomi. I do not like hospitals. Or nursing homes."

Naomi chuckled. "Who does?"

Rosa hovered near in case her grandmother needed her.

Consuela moved the walker and haltingly covered the few yards to the back door. There had been a frost this morning and in the shade the grass still crunched with each footstep. After the hot August, the swiftly cold September had shocked everyone.

Marc hurried forward to open the door. Consuela entered the back porch and then moved into the kitchen. While Naomi went back to drive her car into the garage, Rosa walked past Marc. She wobbled and brushed against him.

He took her arm. "Are you all right?"

All the fatigue and worry rolled into a hot tight ball in her middle. The temptation to lean against him and let him hold her—till she could face all this—tried to overwhelm her. She moved forward away from him.

"A year ago my brother and I enlarged this doorway and the one to the kitchen," Marc said. "And the door to my gram's bathroom and put in one of those new tubs that have the side that swings out. And we put hand grips on the bathroom wall, too. We're handicapped accessible."

"I wish my apartment had been," Rosa muttered.

"Well, your new house will be," Marc said. "Even before this happened, when I realized your grandmother would be living with you, I made sure that your doors are wider than usual and your bathroom will have a shower separate from the tub. And the shower will have built-in hand grips."

Rosa found she couldn't say anything. She hadn't thought of any of these things, but this kind man had.

"You are a good man," Consuela said. "You did this for your *abuela,* too?"

Marc looked embarrassed by the praise. "My brother and I were just doing some maintenance and updating." He shrugged. "You should thank my mom. She's the one who suggested these changes. She said it would be wise to make it possible for my grandmother to stay in her own home, no matter what came down the road."

Rosa loved how he side-stepped praise.

Naomi hurried inside. "Consuela, I've put one of my padded dining room chairs with arms here in the living room for you like the occupational therapist suggested. I only have one bedroom so we have a bed set up in here for you."

Consuela lowered herself into the chair provided and began to weep. "You are such good people. *Dios te bendiga.* God bless you."

Rosa patted Consuela's shoulder, holding back tears. How could she ever repay this kindness? Only God could.

On Saturday morning, Marc drove to the Habitat site, eager to make progress on Rosa's house. Unfortunately, fewer and fewer volunteers had been able to come in the past two weeks. The chill of this early fall had deepened and a few high maple leaves had changed red and yellow overnight. He parked on New Friends Street and was disappointed to see so few cars in front of Rosa's house.

Frustration ate at him. *I wanted Rosa moved in before Halloween.* Approaching the back door, he heard voices inside and let himself into what would be the kitchen.

Eleanor Washburn was there already with only a few workers, mostly retired people. Rosa was kneeling by a large coffeepot which she was plugging in. "Coffee will be ready soon," she said in an obvious attempt at cheerfulness.

Marc propped himself against one of the studs in the open walls. "I was hoping we'd have some more people come. I wanted to see if we could get most of the wallboard up today."

Eleanor pulled out her cell phone. "I'll call a few people and see—"

The kitchen door opened. Bud, Tracy, Luke, Jill and her dad, all in work clothing, walked in one by one.

Marc's eyebrows rose, his mouth opened.

"Did we surprise you?" Jill asked. "We thought the five of us could move things along."

Grinning, Marc slapped Luke on the back.

Rosa stood up. She burst into tears. "Everyone has been so good."

Marc was relieved when Tracy and Jill went over to comfort Rosa. His dad came up to him. "I hear you're the ramrod on this job. So what are we doing today, boss?"

"Wallboard." Marc couldn't stop grinning. He knew how fast and how hard his brother and dad could work.

"Ah, I love putting up walls," Luke said. Everyone laughed. "And for sure we'll all get our workouts today."

Marc moved into action, organizing and explaining. But his true attention focused on the sweet smile curving Rosa's lips. He recalled them brushing his. *Rosa, what can I do to keep away from you? Especially when I don't want to.*

Only a glimmer of sunset lingered on the horizon. October was half over before Rosa had time to take a break, really just stop and think. While running back and forth between work, school, her apartment and Naomi's house where Consuela still stayed, she had managed to keep up with school and work—just barely.

Tonight was a special day in the Chambers's family. Marc's father, Bud, and Luke had both been born on October 18. She'd been invited to the joint birthday celebration, which was a bonfire and wiener roast.

Looking for some fun, she had come; however, the letter in her pocket wouldn't let her relax. Tense and trying to hide this, she stood in Naomi's backyard near what had been a vegetable garden. A few killing frosts had reduced the garden to broken and withered stems.

With Johnny hovering near, Luke and Marc were sharpening long, thin willow branches that they had cut from the bank of a nearby creek. Johnny with Amigo at his side watched the two men.

In the fading light, she couldn't take her eyes from Marc. In the last of the sun, his silhouette appeared solid, reassuringly substantial. He was down on one knee. An old illustration from a book cover came to mind—a Medieval knight on one knee pledging his honor.

"Can I do that?" Johnny asking, bringing her back to the present.

"Sure," Marc replied, pulling Johnny to stand in front of him. Just as he had the day he'd taught him how to hammer in a nail, Marc stooped and placed Johnny's hands within his. This simple act of kindness drew Rosa toward Marc. He was kindhearted and steadfast. He was not Trent. At this thought, her heart contracted, hurting her.

"This one's end has been sharpened enough. Help me strip the bark." He let Johnny help him as he ran the pocket knife away from them, down the willow sapling, stripping the bark.

"Why do we have to take the bark off?" Johnny asked.

"So it doesn't burn while we're using these to roast wieners," Marc replied.

Rosa listened to this very ordinary exchange—a man teaching a boy. How could Trent have had the gall to pay a lawyer to write this letter to her? She burned with fresh resentment.

"And marshmallows," Luke added. "After wieners, we can roast marshmallows and make s'mores."

"S'mores?" Johnny asked.

"Yeah," Luke replied, "we roast the marshmallows then we put them between graham crackers and a chocolate bar. It all melts together. Delicious."

Johnny whooped, then settled into the task of helping Marc strip the bark.

Rosa remained back from the three. These tender moments consoled her. Anyone could see Johnny soaked in this time with Marc and Luke. He's happy, she thought, her mother's heart glad yet sad. It hurt though—like standing at the entrance of Disney World and not having the price of a ticket. This thought of Florida where Trent lived did nothing to ease her tension.

She moved closer to Marc, seeking his strength. *I won't think of that. Not tonight. Tonight I will have fun and enjoy watching my son be happy. I will not let this event be spoiled.*

Bud and Tracy came through the nearby lane that linked the two farms. "Rosa!" Tracy called out. "So happy you could come!"

Rosa waved, remembering how these two had helped her out. "My pleasure. Happy birthday, Bud!"

A car pulled into the drive and another. More guests began pouring out of the cars. At Naomi's nearby burn pit, Bud and Luke started arranging firewood from a stack behind the garage for the bonfire.

Rosa hovered, ready to help, staying near Marc without doing it in a noticeable way.

The cornfields around Naomi's yard had been harvested. The early autumn had been dry and the farmers had been relieved to start the harvest in good time. Soon Bud lit the kindling and flames lapped up the midnight-blue horizon. The three dogs in their dog run barked occasionally, the sound loud in the country peace.

Rosa saw her grandmother shuffling with her walker

toward them. Naomi walked beside her, dragging Consuela's chair. This chair had arms for the support Consuela needed whenever she must get up again. Rosa hurried forward to take the chair as did Marc.

But another guest reached Naomi first and carried the chair near the ring of rocks around the burn pit. When he came close to the fire, Rosa recognized him. It was Jill's father. He greeted her with a smile. "Rosa, how are you tonight?"

"Fine." She faced Tom but Marc's nearness made her aware of everything keenly—the crackling fire, the happy voices, Marc's shoulder just inches from hers.

Then Jill arrived at the chair with Naomi and Consuela. "Your grandmother is doing so well," Jill crowed. "I can't believe she can walk this well only a month after having her hip replaced."

"*Dios es bueno.* God is good," Consuela said, sitting down in her chair. "And so is this family. I am very grateful for all the help…"

Consuela's words brought moisture to Rosa's eyes. Such good people.

"Oh, you'd do the same for us," Naomi interrupted. "I need help carrying out the hot dogs and chips and cake and well, the whole shebang really."

"I'll help," Rosa said in unison with Jill. Rosa was glad to have something to distract her unruly mind. The two of them hurried inside and carried out the food to the picnic table which already had been set with jack-o'-lantern-decorated paper plates, matching napkins and cups and white plastic flatware. The night air had sharpened, moving them toward the fire. The bonfire in the burn pit crackled and sent up cheery sparks against the dark sky.

Then Jill moved to Luke and took his arm in both her

hands. He leaned over and kissed her cheek. Jill responded in kind.

Rosa glimpsed the looks on both their faces, highlighted by the fire. Both Jill and Luke shone with the look of love.

Two reactions clashed inside Rosa—gladness and a pinch of envy. She hoped only good things for these two good people. *But I want to be loved like that, too. Is that wrong, Father?*

Johnny ran up to her. "Did you see me? I did one of the willow sticks we're going to cook with. Did you see me?"

"Yes, I did." She ruffled her son's very short bangs. Marc had taken him for his first professional haircut. Johnny looked as clean-cut as Marc did now.

As if he heard this thought, Marc appeared. "How are you tonight?"

"Fine," she said, though the letter bothered her like nagging back pain. She looked to his face by the firelight, hoping his presence could banish her hard anger.

Suddenly Tracy let out a shout. Every head turned toward her. "I can't believe it!" she exclaimed.

Rosa halted. Only one thing could make Tracy sound this thrilled. Somehow Rosa knew what was coming. She wanted to be happy for Jill and Luke. But she could feel herself freezing into place as if her veins had all been infused with ice water.

Chapter Eight

⤳

While Marc held Johnny to him, he looked toward Rosa. He saw only her profile in the dark beyond the light. Somehow the way she was standing warned him away. What was going on within her? He looked back at his mom. Tracy lifted Jill's left hand and the firelight caught the diamond. It sparkled, mesmerizing. For a moment, everyone gawked. Then Tracy pulled Jill into her arms for a boisterous rocking hug.

Marc stayed where he was as did Rosa. However, they were the only two that did so. The other guests gathered around Luke and Jill. More hugging, some backslapping, cascades of laughter, squeals of joy. In the flickering firelight, Luke stood beside his bride-to-be, tall and proud.

Two conflicting reactions vied within Marc like knives cutting across each other. *I'm happy for you, Luke, but I'm so alone. I want a wife. I want a life, a family as much as you do.* The wrenching confession revealed a yawning void within him. He stared down into his deep, aching loneliness.

"But it's so sudden!" Tracy called out, evidently able finally to speak again.

"Not really," Luke said. "I knew right away, the first time I talked to her."

Jill moved to stand closer to Luke, pressing against his arm. "It was love at first talk." Everyone laughed.

Marc forced a grin, unhappy with his mixed reaction. *This is about Luke, not about me and my sorry self. Suck it up, Chambers.* He glanced down at Johnny and was surprised to see the boy's troubled expression. And in the shadows away from the fire, Rosa looked frozen in place. *So I'm not the only one who's shaken up by this. But Johnny? Why?*

"When is the wedding to be?" Naomi asked, holding Consuela's hand. Consuela had remained seated and both grandmothers were beaming.

"New Year's Eve afternoon," Jill said.

"New Year's Eve?" Tracy gasped, her hands flying to her mouth. "So soon?"

Jill looked up at Luke, winking. "Yes. We've already reserved my church and we'll have the reception there, too, in the basement."

"We'll start the new year as man and wife," Luke said, his chest expanding visibly.

So soon? Marc throttled back the turbulent reactions to this announcement. He forced himself over the few feet to shake Luke's hand and slap his back. *I am happy for you, Luke. I am.* Johnny followed Marc and now leaned against him, turning his face into Marc's waist. How could this news be bothering Johnny? Why?

"But so soon?" Tracy repeated, still showing shock with widening eyes. "That's just a little over two months. How will we have time to get our dresses and do a bridal shower—"

"You and Bud eloped to Vegas as I recall," Naomi commented dryly.

"You eloped to Las Vegas?" Jill gawked at them.

Consuela chuckled, exchanging knowing glances with Naomi. "*El amor no espera a nadie.* Love waits for no man."

Marc followed the telling of the old family story as if listening to a distant radio program. He was more aware of his own ambivalence and of Johnny hugging him tight. He patted the child's back.

Tracy pursed her lips and looked chagrined at Naomi's reminder of her impetuous marriage. "What can I say—it was the 1970s." His mom made a face. "Okay, I have no right to talk. Thank you for reminding me, Naomi."

Naomi laughed. "I wasn't scolding. I was merely pointing out that true love often doesn't wait for elaborate plans. We'll find dresses and so will Jill."

"I'm going to wear my mother's wedding dress," Jill announced.

"If you need alterations, I will do it," Consuela spoke up. "I can still sew even with this new hip."

Jill went over to Consuela where she sat and took her hand. "Thank you. It would mean a lot to me to have a friend do it. And since Marc will be best man, I want Rosa to be a bridesmaid."

Jill turned to Rosa. "You will, won't you? My favorite cousin will be my maid of honor. But since you double-dated with us the first time we met face to face, I think it's fitting to have you as a bridesmaid."

Rosa gave a stiff nod.

Marc gazed at her and guessed that this invitation to be one of the wedding party had caught Rosa off guard, too. Johnny wrapped his arms around Marc's waist tighter. Marc rubbed the boy's back. *What's wrong, Johnny?*

"Well, this is all very nice, but I'm in the mood to roast

a few hot dogs," Naomi announced. "Anyway good news always gives me an appetite."

"Any news gives you an appetite, Mom," Bud called out. Laughter followed. The gathering moved to surround the blazing fire within the circle of rocks.

Rosa drew farther away from the light, glad to be able to move. If she didn't get away, she wouldn't be able to hold in the hurt in front of everyone. Under the cover of darkness, the happy chatter of the guests and the meat sizzling over the fire, she slipped away. She took refuge in Naomi's dimly lit kitchen.

She gripped the counter around the sink and stared out the window at the fire. The dark shapes moved around it, all backlit by the golden-orange flames. Fierce and fast, emotions slashed through her. Hot tears welled up, scalding her as they streamed down her face. Jill and Luke would live happily ever after while she...The horrible letter burned in her pocket. Why hadn't she torn it into pieces and buried it in her trash?

Outside, Marc sat in a lawn chair. He let Johnny face the fire. But to keep him from getting too near the fire, Marc tucked Johnny between his thighs. Arms outstretched, he skewered a hotdog on the boy's willow stick and handed it to him.

Johnny put his wiener right over the orange flames. Marc looked around for Rosa and then back again. "Johnny, turn your dog over and move it a little way from the direct flame. Otherwise you'll end up with a wiener burned on the outside and cold on the inside."

"Like this?" Johnny asked, gazing into the flames pensively.

"Yeah, that's just right." Marc glanced around, trying not to appear to be looking for Rosa. The last few minutes had been rough not only for him but also Rosa and Johnny.

Marc could hear Johnny's unhappiness in his voice. Marc wanted to make sure Rosa was all right. *And now I can't see her.*

Naomi came over and leaned close to Marc's ear. "Rosa went into my apartment. Go see what she needs."

Marc exchanged glances with his grandmother by the golden firelight. Did she sense something wrong, too? He hoped she hadn't picked up on any of his turmoil. "Johnny," Marc said, "Naomi is going to help you cook your hot dog."

Johnny looked up, worry dragging down his eyes and mouth. "What's wrong?"

"Nothing." Marc squeezed his shoulder. *I hope.* "I have to go get something. Here, Naomi, take my place."

Marc stood up and tried not to call attention to his retreat inside. Leaving the crackling fire and the cheerful voices behind, he entered Naomi's quiet kitchen. The only light on was the one over the stove. Silent, Rosa stood at the sink, gazing out the window.

"Are you all right?" he asked, wary, hesitant.

Rosa whirled around and then sagged against the kitchen counter, glad it wasn't anyone else. *Marc.* Yet she did not want to be alone with Marc now; she longed to throw herself into his arms and feel his strength envelop her. Somehow the letter had stripped away her outer shell. She was exposed, defenseless.

"Sorry," Marc murmured, "I didn't mean to surprise you." He moved toward her, trying to gauge her mood. "Did you need something?" *Need me?*

"No, no." She withdrew from him, wrapping her arms around herself. *I'm too vulnerable. Stay away.*

He tried to think of how to bring up what was uppermost in his mind, Luke's engagement to Jill. *But maybe Rosa doesn't want to talk about that, either.* Could that alone explain her retreating here? "Rosa?" he ventured to say.

She looked into Marc's shadowed face, yearning for his touch. She tightened her tight grip on herself.

The desire to pull Rosa close and hold her nearly overcame Marc's caution. "Are you all right?" he asked again, moving still closer to her in the dim light.

Too many answers came bubbling up. She couldn't speak. She looked away.

"Is it the engagement?" Marc found it hard to draw breath. His eyes adjusted and now picked up the added glow from the back porch light. Rosa's face came into focus.

"It surprised me," Rosa admitted. She looked up, blinking rapidly to keep tears at bay.

"Me, too." *She's crying.* Marc gripped the back of a kitchen chair and laid the other hand on the counter to keep them from reaching for her. "I mean, *man,* that was fast."

"They must be in love." Rosa leaned against the counter. A tight ball of misery lodged right over her heart.

"I guess." Marc couldn't take much more of this enforced restraint. His grip on the chair back had turned his knuckles white. And this conversation was going nowhere on the fast track. He took a chance. "Do you need anything, Rosa?"

"No. We better go back." Rosa said these words, even while she imagined laying her head against Marc's chest and pouring out all the hurt inside her.

"Okay." He didn't move.

She didn't move. The long moment hung between them.

Then breaking free, she headed past him out the door.

He nearly stopped her with a hand on her arm. Nonetheless, he let her go.

And she was grateful. Outside the cleansing frosty night

air filled her lungs. But her heart remained mired in murky heartache and resentment. She tried to shake these unloving feelings without success. She forced a smile, a false and cold and terrible mask.

Hours of the outdoor birthday celebration crept past. Rosa suffered each minute as an hour. When would it end? Leaning against the tree which supported the tire swing, Rosa stayed out of the circle of light. Everyone else was either sitting on half-log benches around the burn pit or in lawn chairs.

She'd managed to choke down a hotdog to stop people from urging her to eat. And now she'd never be able to eat one again without recalling this excruciating evening of the "letter." To her, all the laughter and happy family chatter had been like chewing glass.

Then the long torturous evening was finally, finally coming to an end. A few neighbors had risen to say their thanks and goodnights.

"Johnny!" Rosa called, walking toward the fire. Her pulse sped up now that escape was within reach. "It's time to go home." *At last.*

Johnny was sprawled back on Bud's lap as Bud lingered in one of the lawn chairs around the fire.

She approached them. "Come on, Johnny." She forced a cheerful tone. "Time for us to head home."

"No," her son said, turning and wrapping his arms around Bud's waist. "I want to stay here with Marc and Amigo."

"Johnny," she said, trying to sound patient, even as her thin patience slipped through her fingers. "Marc's been very nice to have you spend nights here with him, but tonight you're coming home with me."

"No."

Rosa's lips pressed tightly together, holding back sharp words. "Johnny, I said it's time to go."

"No."

"Johnny."

"No!"

Rosa heard the high hysterical edge to her son's voice. He was definitely overtired. And an overtired child could not behave well nor respond to reason. She knew that. But her forbearance was hanging by a single spider web thread. "Johnny—"

"No!" Her son leaped off Bud's lap and pelted toward Naomi's back door.

Rosa closed her eyes, trying to withstand the onslaught of surging frustration, now crashing against her festering resentment over the letter. And she was completely depleted, fresh out of patience, sucked dry. *I can't do this tonight. I can't.*

But mothers had to bear everything. No days off for moms. She turned and began trudging toward Naomi's door as if wading through deep wet snow. *I'm so tired, Father. Help.*

When she reached the door, Johnny was on the other side—out of her reach. By the light over the back door and through its window, she saw he was prepared for war. With both hands, he'd clasped the knob in a death grip. With his feet braced against the bottom of the door, he was leaning back, pulling his whole body weight against the door. This made it impossible for her to open it.

"Johnny, stop this right now," she snapped along with the thread of her patience. "Now."

"No!" Johnny yelled back.

Tracy appeared at her elbow. "He's obviously overdone. Why don't you let him stay tonight? You've had a rough month running back and forth with your grandmother."

Tracy laid a restraining hand on Rosa's shoulder. "You look so exhausted. Go home and go to bed. Relax for a night. If Marc doesn't want him tonight, we'll take Johnny home with us. He can bunk in with Luke."

"No, I'll keep him," Marc said, arriving beside his mother, "Rosa, Mom's right. You do look exhausted. I'll keep Johnny overnight and bring him to you tomorrow morning."

Rosa wanted to scream, *He's my son! He has to obey me!*

"Listen to them, dear," Naomi said, joining the group. "You need a break and obviously Johnny does, too. This has all been a very confusing time for him."

Rosa looked at Johnny's defiant face. She felt herself losing control just as he had. Before she embarrassed herself by screaming in frustration, she conceded. "Okay. Call me in the morning." She turned and made a quick getaway, jogging to her car. Consuela called, "Good night!" Rosa didn't slow up. Angry words hovered just over her tongue, ready to spill over.

She backed out of the drive and headed home. Now the tears poured down her face. She hated them. And even more she hated the lost feeling and then the anger that had come when she'd opened the awful letter. Would her wrong choice at sixteen dog her and her son for the rest of their lives?

Marc watched Rosa rush to her car and drive off. Something more than fatigue and Luke and Jill's engagement had to be fueling this. He hoped he'd made the right decision to let her drive herself home.

"She looked worn out," Tracy said.

He nodded, feeling like a traitor for not trying to find out what was the matter earlier in the kitchen. Marc looked through the window at the naughty, unhappy boy. "Johnny, open the door. Now."

Reluctantly, as if he knew how much trouble he was in, Johnny obeyed. The door inched open. Then he burst into tears and barreled into Marc's arms. "I'm sorry." The boy began to cry in an hysterical, disjointed way. "I'm sorry."

Marc folded Johnny in his arms and went inside. As he carried him up the stairs, he patted the boy's back. The evening had been sharply unsettling for the three of them, Rosa, Johnny and himself. All the turbulence he'd hidden over the past hours had chafed him raw. *But I'm happy for Luke. I am.*

He heard the door open downstairs and Naomi called up, "Here's what the boy needs!" Barking full blast, Amigo bounded inside and clattered up the steps to Marc's apartment.

"Amigo," Johnny stuttered between sobs, reaching for the dog.

Marc sat down on the couch where Johnny slept when visiting. Johnny slid to his knees. Amigo panted beside the boy, licking his face, wriggling with happiness.

"I'll go get your sleeping bag," Marc said, feeling at least a hundred years old.

Knuckling his eyes, Johnny nodded. A stray sob escaped him. Marc pulled him close for a quick hug and then left. When Marc returned, he helped the boy change into his pajamas and then took him to the bathroom to brush his teeth. Amigo trailed after them.

Afterward, Marc lifted Johnny into his arms and carried him. Still crying in a helpless exhausted way, Johnny slid into the Green Bay Packer's green-and-gold sleeping bag.

"Now go to sleep." Marc touched the child's forehead.

"I don't want to go home," Johnny mumbled. "Luke is

gonna marry Jill. I want you to marry my mom. And then we could live together. I wouldn't ever have to go home, go away."

Johnny sounded completely distraught and nearly asleep. But his words hit Marc squarely. So that was what had caused Johnny's strange reaction. Sitting beside the boy, Marc rubbed Johnny's back and murmured repeatedly, "Go to sleep. Everything will be all right in the morning. Promise."

Finally the boy stopped hiccupping and crying. After turning three times, Amigo made himself comfortable on Johnny's feet. Amigo sighed, happy with his boy.

Marc felt the child's body relax into sleep. Marc remained on the edge of the couch, gazing at Johnny. Johnny had said, *Luke is marrying Jill. I want you to marry my mom.* Johnny deserved a father. But was Marc the man who should fill that role? Still haunted by nightmares, could he measure up? *Lord, help Johnny, help Rosa, help me...*

Rosa unlocked the door of her apartment. Closing and locking the door behind her, she dropped her purse onto the floor and fell forward onto the sofa. Sorrow and hurt weighed on her like brick and mortar. For once, she was alone and didn't have to be brave for anyone else. She let all the hurt gush out. Sobs shook, wrenched her whole body. The letter had ripped open the past wound of Trent's rejection of her and Johnny, letting its poison sting and sear her once more. She lay, weeping, weeping.

At last, she was cried out, drained. She lay on her stomach in the dark apartment, gazing at the small round illuminated clock on the stove. Nearly eleven o'clock. And she was too weak to get up and go through even the nightly routine of ending the day. Overhead, footsteps and someone's pipes gurgled. She lay unmoving, spent.

"I know I have a lot to be grateful for," Rosa, alone in the dark, said to God. "We're about to move into a house of our own. Johnny's in good health. My grandfather is being well cared for and so is Consuela. I'm going to school. But I'm so tired, Father. So tired of going it alone. Of never having anyone here to share the load with, share the joy with. I long for a deep voice, calling my name and Johnny's. I want a man's love, Father. A good man. I want to be able to give all the love in my heart to a good man. A faithful man."

Marc's face came to mind. She acknowledged the fact that she was in love with him. But was he in love with her? Did that matter if he was still wounded from the accident? She recalled those moments in his pickup the day at school that Caroline Mason's sister had spoken to him. Had he healed? Would he ever be able to love without guilt?

She knew that none of this mattered. She was going to love him anyway. Nevertheless, that wouldn't solve her problems with Trent and his lousy letter.

Rosa woke up still facedown on the couch. She hadn't moved all night. Washed out and stiff, she tried to recall why her heart felt filled with hardening cement. *The letter. Of course.* More evidence of how little Trent valued her or his firstborn son.

She rolled onto her back and stared at the dingy white popcorn ceiling. *What am I going to do?*

The image of Eleanor Washburn popped into her mind. *That's who I should call. I need a lawyer and she's a lawyer.* Trent had hired a lawyer to write this nasty letter. *I can hire one, too.* She rolled onto her feet and went to the wall phone in the kitchen. After dialing Eleanor's number, she sat down at their tiny table. Eleanor came on the line.

The sound of this take-charge woman's voice bolstered Rosa's confidence. "Good morning, this is Rosa Santos. Eleanor, I need a lawyer. Can you help me?"

The next morning had dawned as one of those bright, chilly autumn days that made Marc glad to be alive. With not a second to spare, he arrived near Rosa's apartment in time to get Johnny on the school bus. After waving Johnny off, Marc knocked on Rosa's apartment door. Today he'd push to find out what had upset her last night. He couldn't believe it was only Jill and Luke's engagement. Rosa wasn't like that.

She opened her door. "Hi, come on in."

Marc tried to measure her mood. He wanted to say, "You sound better this morning." But on second thought, he didn't know if he should even mention last night. After the accident, he hadn't liked it when people kept asking him over and over, "How are you?"

"I made it to the bus," he said, testing this morning's emotional waters, "just in time to get Johnny on it."

Rosa leaned forward and rested her head on his chest. Her touch was pure bliss. His heart thudded with sudden force. Yet before he could put an arm around her, she backed away.

"Come in. I've made coffee." She wouldn't meet his eyes then.

He entered the apartment, experiencing an odd hesitance. He'd never been here, just the two of them alone before. Rosa sounded better. What had happened to turn things around?

"Did Johnny give you any more trouble last night?" she asked, leading him the short way to the small kitchen table.

"No, he realized that he was in trouble, big-time. He

brushed his teeth, got into his pj's and went to sleep." *And he wants me to marry you.* The thought had power. Marc experienced an odd sensation almost as if his heart was being drawn from him toward her. *Rosa, could you love me?*

"Thanks for taking Johnny for the night." She poured him a Green Bay mug of coffee and motioned him to sit opposite her. The fragrance of fresh coffee filled the tiny kitchen. "I'm glad you were able to deal with him. It always seems that when I am totally stressed out, that's when he gets the same way."

Stressed out? Not by the announcement of the engagement, Rosa. What's bothering you? Marc wrapped his freezing hands around the heavy mug. "Kids don't know how to take a break. At least, that's what my mom said Luke and I used to do—go full speed and then crash. It's just kids."

She gave him a smile with only a sprinkle of amusement. "Don't be afraid of me, Marc. I'm better today." She paused as if waiting for something. Then she handed him a crumpled letter that had been lying on the table. "Read this and you'll understand why I was so tense last night."

He scanned the very official-looking letter which asked that Trent's monthly child support payment for Johnny be reduced. Marc hit the table with his palm. "Man! He's got some nerve."

Rosa somehow made a sound that both agreed with him and also chastised Johnny's natural father. "I called Eleanor Washburn this morning at her law office. She's going to respond to Trent's letter. Instead of decreasing the amount, she has encouraged me to ask for an increase. Johnny's getting older and needs more financial support, not less."

"Good for you." He sipped his hot coffee, still wishing he could kick Trent around the block a few times.

"I'm sorry that I let this get me down." She paused with her mug in front of her mouth. "It's because…it's because I think this request to decrease Johnny's support comes from the fact that Trent wants more money for the new baby that's coming."

Her words stoked Marc's irritation. *Trent, you are a jerk.*

She took a sip and then gave him a fierce look. "I won't have Johnny slighted or treated as less important just because Trent decided he didn't want the consequences of our…" She paused again, pressing her lips tight. "When Trent asked me out in high school, I was so flattered. I mean, he was class president, on the football team. I guess I was dazzled that he'd be interested in me. I made a poor decision to become sexually active in high school. Trent made promises he didn't mean or couldn't keep. I wish I had followed God's plan of waiting till marriage." She began dusting a few particles of salt from the tabletop.

Marc nodded. "You deserve better."

She shook her head. "I knew I was doing wrong. *Johnny* deserves better. I'm doing my best—"

"You deserve better," Marc insisted, irritation with Trent pulsing through his veins. "And you've done a great job with him. He's a good kid, well behaved and honest."

"With an occasional lapse." She gave him a half smile. But her eyes completed it, crinkling up.

The tight invisible band around his chest loosened. He grinned in return. His hand tingled wanting to reach for Rosa's so near his. Finally, he bravely placed his hand over hers. "Is there any way I can help?"

She didn't take her hand away. "You've already helped."

Their hands warmed each other. He gazed into her eyes, memorizing each detail of her wing-like brows, the black center of her deep brown iris. He was afraid to push matters. Just holding her hand had been audacious. To say the words of love he wanted to voice, to speak them in the open air, with honesty and freedom…. *It's too soon. Too soon. For both of us.*

Chapter Nine

In the morning, Rosa arrived at her Habitat house, ready to work. While waiting, she busied herself making another large pot of coffee. Then Naomi, followed by Marc, walked into the kitchen. The sight of him tripped her pulse to speed up.

"Where is everybody?" Naomi asked.

Rosa shrugged, downhearted. From outside came the sudden sound of car doors. All three of them turned to look out the window. And then came a knock at the side door. Rosa opened it and then stepped back with a gasp. Her mouth opened wide. She recognized her pastor, his wife, their teenaged sons, followed by two more friends from church.

"We heard you needed some painters today," the tall pastor with silvered hair announced with a grin. "We brought our own rollers and brushes." He waved a new paint roller. "Where do we start?"

Rosa covered her mouth with her hand. For a few moments, she couldn't speak. "I didn't expect this." *I don't deserve this.*

"We're sorry we haven't come out before to help," he said. "But life gets so busy. And I'm not much of a carpenter. However, I do know which end of a brush to hold."

Smiling, Marc came forward and shook the pastor's hand. "You've come to the right place." He motioned down the hallway toward the three bedrooms. "I'll need people in each room to mask the woodwork, edge and then paint."

Rosa watched as some of her church family, all dressed in work clothing, claimed rooms to paint. In the midst of the abundant banter and laughter, Rosa was humbled and deeply touched.

"Well, it certainly got crowded in here," Naomi crowed as she headed toward the large bathroom behind the kitchen, her area to paint.

The question of why Eleanor hadn't come yet niggled at the back of Rosa's mind. She looked to Marc, wondering why Eleanor hadn't, at least, called. But being near Marc distracted her. He looked so competent, so kind. His face always crinkled into that smile she loved to see. She nearly said this but substituted, "I didn't expect them...I didn't know..."

Marc grinned at her. "I know, but it was just what we both needed for a change. A good surprise. Now, Rosa, you are going to help me hang your kitchen cabinets." He motioned grandly toward the large cardboard boxes scattered around the empty living room.

Rosa heard his no-nonsense tone and immediately her worries lifted. He was taking charge and she liked it. If Marc put her kitchen together, it would be done right. But worry tugged again. *Eleanor, why aren't you here this morning?*

"I wonder where our fearless leader is," Marc said, putting her concern into words.

"I was wondering that, too," she said, looking toward the door. She shook her head at her own foolishness. Did she expect Eleanor to appear just because they had mentioned her name? Still, Rosa's midsection churned with uncertainty.

Marc pulled out a box cutter and began opening boxes. Soon her beautiful dark walnut cabinets sat around the living room.

Rosa's cell phone rang. She jerked it from her pocket.

"Rosa," the brisk voice on the line said, "Eleanor here."

Relief mixed with hurt rushed up and knotted inside Rosa. "Eleanor—"

The lawyer cut her off. "I've been delayed at the office. I'm waiting to hear back from Trent's lawyer. He said he would call this morning. And I don't want to give him any reason for complaint. I would have the call forwarded to my cell phone so I could be there to move work along. But I have all your papers here and might need them for reference."

"That's fine," Rosa said, trying to feel fine. "My pastor and his family have come to paint," Rosa said. Her mind still rebelled at having to go through this bad business with Trent. Why had he stirred matters up? *I wouldn't have caused him trouble.* She tried to close her mind to Trent and his petty meanness.

"I'll come as soon as I can." Eleanor hung up before Rosa could mention the latest of what Trent had done or rather left undone.

Rosa closed her phone and slipped it into her pocket, suddenly feeling lost. She had wanted to tell Eleanor not to spend too much time on this thing with Trent. After all, she wasn't paying Eleanor. *I don't want to take advantage of her good nature.*

In spite of her dark mood, Rosa smiled stiffly, not wishing to involve Marc any further in her problems. She appreciated his support but would not impose on it, especially since she was beginning to depend on him. *I can't do that. The house is nearly done and then he will not be around as much.* "How can I help, Marc?"

He began hefting the upper cabinets to the floor below the places for each and motioned for her to join in. Unable to lift the heavy walnut cabinets, Rosa "walked" several over and then waited to see what she needed to do next to help him.

"These are really nice," he said, surveying them.

"They were a bit more expensive," Rosa admitted, "but Eleanor encouraged me to get these instead of the cheaper ones." She still didn't feel comfortable with this decision.

"Stop beating yourself up about the expense," Marc urged. "These will last you a lifetime. Good wood lasts. You don't want the cheap ones that won't stand up to daily use."

She looked at him, silently repeating his words. She was beating herself up over this and so much more. "Okay." Then she turned away, unexpected tears smarting in her eyes. *I don't deserve this. All these good people taking time and effort to help me.*

Then Marc appeared at her elbow. "What's the matter?"

"I don't deserve all this," she said, unable to stop the words from coming.

"That's just a crazy way to think, Rosa," he said in a kind tone. He touched her arm gently. "You are a good person, a wonderful mother. Why shouldn't people help you? You are always ready to help someone else."

She shook her head, forcing back this display of emotion. She shuddered once as if suddenly freezing. "I don't know. I—"

"I know," he said firmly, "you've been through a lot

and carried a heavy load for a long time. But that's all past and this is the present, okay?" He cupped her elbow in one hand.

His gentle touch and reassuring words deepened her reaction to him, the pull to move closer. She forced herself not to turn to him and lean against him. *Father, I don't deserve this house. I don't deserve all these people coming to help me, especially this good man. But thank You. Thank You. And please don't let Trent ruin my joy in this blessing. Bring Trent's support check soon. Guard my heart against resentment.*

A few days later on a cold but sunny morning, Rosa stood outside her house. Moving in day had arrived. Snug in her red University of Wisconsin hoodie, she couldn't stop looking at her house, all finished. After she was all moved in, there would be a potluck with the volunteers in the basement. Rosa gazed at the realization of a dream she hadn't expected to ever come true.

She and her family had always lived in houses which belonged to others. *I should be happy.* Yet a block of granite sat on her lungs. Trent had managed to cause her to continue worrying on this special day. *I hate that.* And she hated that she had put off telling Eleanor why.

Rosa dreaded even voicing Trent's name. Just thinking about him covered her sun with thick angry clouds. She lifted her chin. *I'll tell Eleanor. Today.*

Now at the curb, she admired her finished house. It was sided with a no-upkeep siding which looked like wood and her door was a dark pine green and the trim a lighter shade of the same green. Satisfaction rolled through her, strong and positive.

"It really looks nice, doesn't it?" Naomi said, standing beside her. Other people began arriving, many carrying fragrant Crock-Pots and casserole dishes to plug in on the kitchen counter. When Eleanor came out onto the front stoop, Rosa approached her. But Rosa didn't want to say what she needed here in front of everyone. Rosa held back the worry until she could catch a private moment with her lawyer.

In swift order, Eleanor had the moving-in organized. The volunteers with good backs lined up and carried the largest boxes and Rosa's few pieces of furniture to the specified rooms.

A large delivery truck pulled up to the curb.

Rosa happened to stop next to Marc.

"Are you expecting new furniture?" he asked with a smile.

"I just ordered a new mattress and box spring," she explained, watching Eleanor for an opportunity to speak to her privately. "I needed a new one because I slept on the sofa bed in our apartment. And that will be in the basement family room."

Then Rosa's breath caught in her throat. She ran forward, "No! No! I didn't order that furniture!"

The delivery men in khaki work clothing halted by the cherrywood dresser they had just unloaded. The larger of the two men, the one who needed a shave badly, looked at Rosa. "No, this is for you, lady. Here, read this." He handed her what looked like an invoice.

She studied it, a line forming between her eyebrows. "There must be some mix-up."

Marc watched Rosa's expression change from irritation to wide-eyed shock. He made his way through the small knots of volunteers to her side and read over her shoulder. The paper didn't look out of order, just a regular delivery invoice but it was for more than a mattress set. "This doesn't make sense."

"There must be some mix-up," Rosa repeated, still looking at the invoice. "Like I told you—I only ordered a mattress and box spring, not a whole bedroom set." She waved the invoice as if scolding it.

She turned to the delivery men. "You need to call your boss. This is a mistake."

"No, it isn't a mistake," the truck driver with the stubbly chin replied. "You're right though, this was a funny one. Somebody called the store, ordered the bedroom set and then sent us an anonymous money order with the price in full."

"What?" This one word came from Rosa and Eleanor almost in unison.

Marc hadn't noticed that Eleanor had come to where he and Rosa were standing by the furniture. He handed her the invoice, but was ignored.

"What store do you work for and what's the number?" Eleanor asked in her don't-try-my-patience lawyer-tone. She whipped out her cell phone. "This might be some scam," she murmured.

The trucker pointed to the side of the truck for the store logo and number. By now, everyone had stopped and come outside to watch the center stage drama. They gathered around Rosa and Marc while Eleanor talked into her cell phone, sounding disbelieving and disgruntled. She snapped her phone shut. "Well, this man is right. It happened just the way he described."

"Just like the doughnuts and coffee we received early on," Naomi added. "But they were paid with cash. I wonder who Rosa's fairy god-person could be." Naomi teased, eyes gleaming with fun.

"It might be you," Marc pointed out.

"No, not me." Naomi shook her head. "What about you?"

The question stung since he'd wanted to do something like this for Rosa. But he didn't have the money to buy furniture like this.

Suddenly he thought of something he could make for Rosa in his grandfather's old woodworking shed. Could he have it done before Thanksgiving for Rosa? It was just what she'd need, too. He began planning right then.

"Hey," the delivery truck driver said, rubbing his chin. "This isn't our last call of the day. Can we get this delivered or what?"

Marc drew Rosa backward out of the path of the delivery men. He glanced around, noticing that even Rosa's new neighbors had come out of their houses to see what all the commotion was all about. And with his own plan shining within him, he didn't feel so bad that a stranger had come to Rosa's rescue. Well not as bad.

"Marc, I don't feel right about accepting this furniture," Rosa said in a voice just for him. She had folded her arms in front of herself.

"Why?" He leaned closer, smelling her sweet scent, something with the fragrance of apples. "You need the furniture, don't you?"

"Yes, but—"

"Accepting an anonymous gift isn't against the law, right?" he continued persuasively. He touched her arm, wishing he could pull her close and give her a hug, but there were too many eyes watching.

"No, but—"

He squeezed her arm instead of hugging her. "Rosa, let it go. God has blessed you. Accept it. Don't be an ungracious receiver."

She bowed her head. "You're right. It's just that—"

"It's just that you have shouldered the responsibility

for so long that it seems funny to have help?" Even as he posed this question, it came to him that he was guilty of the same failing.

He had thought he could recover from the accident all by himself, but God had sent a stray dog to help him sleep at night and a little boy who needed him.

He looked around. If only they were alone, he would have said much more. He pressed her arm again, wishing he could touch her cheek, her hair. He took a deep breath. "We'll talk later, okay?"

Rosa nodded, still looking troubled. "Yes, we better get busy or all my stuff will be put in the wrong closets." She hurried past the delivery men as they came back to carry in another piece of furniture.

Bereft, Marc watched her go. She was moving into her house which meant that he wouldn't be seeing her as much, just glimpses at the local college and at Johnny's soccer practices and games. The lonely thought whistled through him like a cold wind. He watched more furniture being carried in. And he comforted himself, knowing he'd make a surprise for Rosa. Johnny and Rosa had become a part of his family. He wanted them to have only the best of everything. *And I don't want to lose them.* He tried to push this lonely thought away. *I won't lose them—if only the nightmares will stay away.*

That evening Rosa stood at her son's bedroom door. Marc sat on Johnny's bed, talking to him about soccer. She wanted to stand here, watching her son so happy, and savor the moment and then tuck away the memory.

The reality that this was *her* house, hers and Johnny's and her grandmother's lapped over her wave after wave. Still she couldn't take it all in. *This is my home. This is our home.* And nothing that Trent did or didn't do could spoil this moment for her.

She'd finally told Eleanor today that Trent's monthly child support check was over a week late. Eleanor had said that she'd take care of that in a tone that meant business. Well, Trent had asked for whatever he got over this last slight. Another, more poignant thought, however, tugged at her. She pushed it to the back of her mind.

"It's way past your bedtime, Johnny." Marc rose and pulled back the covers. "Climb in and your mom will tuck you in."

"You can tuck me in," Johnny said.

Rosa walked to Marc's side. Her concern over letting Johnny trust Marc tried to ring a warning bell, but not even a distant jingling sounded. She could trust Marc with her son. *Why did I ever think I could trust Trent? All the signs were there if I'd only paid attention.* His bad reputation with other girls had already been established in high school and she'd ignored it.

Thinking of Trent brought back the thought that had plagued her all day. *I shouldn't be thinking of this now.* "We'll both tuck you in, Johnny," she said, making herself smile. She booted Trent out of her mind.

Marc and she pulled up the covers together. She kissed her son's forehead and Marc patted Johnny's shoulder. "Remember to say your prayers," she reminded him.

"I will. I want to thank God for this great house. I love having my own room," Johnny replied, folding his hands and closing his eyes.

Rosa led Marc from the room, switching off the light. Waves of joy and some other emotion she wouldn't identify rushed through. She refused to make a big deal. She paused at her grandmother's door. Consuela was sitting up in bed, reading her Spanish Holy Bible. All three exchanged cheery, "*Buenas noches.*"

"Let's get those dishes washed," Marc said, motioning toward the kitchen.

She covered the few steps with Marc at her heels. "You've done so much already—"

He reached for a new dishcloth lying beside the sink. "I learned how to dry dishes at an early age. Come on."

She gave in and began washing and rinsing the few dishes left over from the potluck. They were soon put away neatly in the new walnut cabinets. Rosa paused to stroke the lovely dark wood and thought of how her mother would have liked them.

Rosa drained the sink and wiped the counter. The mundane chore was wonderful and new. *This is my countertop, my kitchen.* She rested her back against the counter and gazed at the large open concept living/dining room, letting it all sink in. Marc stood beside her, his back against the counter, too.

"I really like the way this all comes together," Marc commented. "In my mom's house, we rarely use the living room even when we have company. She has that big country kitchen and family room at the back. It reminds me of your place. You know a fireplace wouldn't be hard to add to that wall."

His simple kind words pushed her past her point of no return. Rosa turned away to hide the sudden rush of tears.

"Hey," Marc said, turning her toward him, "hey, you don't need to have a fireplace. I just thought it would be nice."

This made her chuckle in the midst of tears. "It's not that, Marc."

"What is it then?" When she didn't answer right away, he tugged her closer. "You can tell me," he whispered.

At these words, her decision not to involve Marc in her regret eased. She took Marc's hand and drew him toward the loveseat one of the volunteers had given her. "I just wish—" she sat and drew him down to sit beside her "—all day I've thought of my mother and wished she could have lived to be in this house. She deserved this, too." Rosa kept his work-roughened hand in hers.

Marc drew her closer and put his arm around her. "When Johnny stayed with me that first night Consuela was in the hospital, he said that his *other* grandmother had not come home from that hospital."

Rosa gazed into his clear straightforward eyes. "Yes, he was only four when she passed away, but he does remember her." She looked down.

"That must have been rough," he murmured. "I…" His voice faded away.

"What is it, Marc?" She looked up at him, concern for him crowding out her own pain.

"You never speak of your father."

She looked away, but told the unhappy truth. "My father left as soon as he knew I was on the way."

Instead of asking more unwelcome questions, Marc drew her closer and kissed her forehead.

He was a man more sensitive than most. Perhaps the accident had given him more understanding of deep sorrow. This drew her to him even more. She knew she shouldn't but she tucked up her feet and nestled into Marc's arms. "I miss my mom, you know?"

"I know. I was really close to my grandfather." He stroked her cheek with his thumb. "I was in high school when he died. In my whole childhood, he never missed a game I played in. Not one."

She rested her head on his shoulder and gazed up into his blue eyes. All the objections to becoming close to Marc, which she had come up with over the past few months, dissolved in this tender moment. She cupped his stubbled cheek. "I'm sorry. Was that Naomi's husband?"

"Yes, my other grandparents died young in an accident. My parents inherited the farm they live on from them. My mom and dad were childhood sweethearts. My dad always says he didn't have to go farther than the next farm to find his true love."

"How sweet." Rosa's throat was closing up.

"I don't get why it's so easy for some to find the one they love and want to marry and others…" He shrugged.

"That's what I was just thinking." She moved her hand along his jaw and then let it rest on his shoulder.

His face began to lower. The exquisite anticipation of his coming kiss crinkled through her, a delightful jittery sensation.

Lower, lower and then his mouth hovered over hers. The last half inch filled her with a tenderness and eagerness she'd never known.

"May I kiss you, Rosa?" he asked.

"Si." That was all she could force from her throat.

His lips claimed hers, his kiss was all she had anticipated. A gentle but insistent caressing. She clung to him, letting this special kiss from this special man form a memory she would never let go.

"Rosa," he breathed, finally lifting his lips from hers.

She blushed and hid her face in the space between his chin and chest.

He lightly kissed her forehead then. "Rosa, you have become very special to me. You and Johnny."

She gazed into his honest eyes then. "It's all too much to take in. This house and you. It's too wonderful."

He kissed her again. "We've both had hard times, but maybe we've turned the corner." He ran a finger around her ear, smoothing back her hair. His touch made her tremble. "Be my girl?"

Her cup had been filled and was overflowing. She nodded. "Be my guy?"

He grinned and nodded. And she knew he was going to kiss her again. And she knew she could trust him not to ask for more. Far back in her brain, a persistent voice scolded her, *You don't deserve this house, much less this man. This won't last.*

She ignored the voice. *God has never let me down. Marc has never let me down. I will trust them.*

On the next Saturday afternoon, Rosa sat in Marc's truck with Johnny between her and Marc. Her heart hummed with happiness, an inviting golden happiness that fit this beautiful golden autumn day.

Marc pulled into the gravel pumpkin farm parking lot and found a place. Switching off the motor, he turned to Johnny and Rosa with a huge grin. "So how big a pumpkin did you say you wanted?"

Johnny rounded his arms and barely touched his fingertips together. "This big."

"I don't know," Marc said, getting out. "If you get one that big, you might fall into it and—plop, you'll be like Peter's wife."

Rosa laughed.

"Who's Peter?" Johnny scrambled down after Marc.

"You'll see." Marc came around and opened her door. He clasped his hands at her waist and swung her down to the gravel lot. She laughed out loud with the joy at his gesture of affection. Her face lifted into a broad smile. She and Marc each took one of Johnny's hands and walked toward the seasonal attraction, Petrie's Pumpkins and Storybook Land. The Petrie Family used cornstalks, pumpkins and tempera paints to depict various fairy tales and nursery rhymes. Marc, Johnny and Rosa walked past several groups of painted pumpkins. Then they paused at "Peter, Peter, Pumpkin Eater."

Reciting the nursery rhyme, Marc pointed to the pumpkin head with a woman's wig protruding from a larger pumpkin. "See that's what will happen to you if you get a pumpkin that's too big."

"Oh, that's just an old nursery rhyme," Johnny replied, entering into the extended joke.

"It looks real to me," Rosa joined in, her heart warm and bursting with gladness. She glanced to her right.

And all her delight disintegrated.

Why did *they* have to be here?

She turned her back to Trent's parents, hoping they wouldn't see her and Johnny. Trent's mother had a sharp tongue as Rosa recalled painfully. She pointed in the opposite direction. "Let's go see Little Jack Horner." *Let's get away from her.*

Marc and Johnny went along with her suggestion. Out of the corner of her eye, Rosa kept track of the people she most wanted to avoid. She hoped that they hadn't planned to come just when Johnny and she were here. Of course, they couldn't have. *They wouldn't have known when we were coming. Stop being paranoid.*

Marc, Johnny and she worked their way through the many displays of decorated pumpkins—Mary with her lamb, Little Bo-Peep, Jack and the Beanstalk. She began to relax. The pumpkin farm was crowded with people. No doubt the ones she wanted to avoid would avoid her by choice, too.

She, Marc and Johnny had finally worked their way

through all the displays and moved on to the acres of pumpkins to choose Johnny's.

"I want the biggest pumpkin we can carry!" Johnny announced, again opening his arms wide to show how big the pumpkin should be. They walked through the ranks of pumpkins. Finally they found one that Johnny thought was big enough.

"You think I can lift that monster?" Marc teased, bracing his low back with both hands. "Oh, Rosa, your son's trying to break my back."

"You." The word was spoken as an accusation.

Rosa recognized that voice, had learned to dread that voice. So she didn't show any reaction, acting as if she'd not heard the woman. "I don't know, Johnny," Rosa said, hoping the woman would go away. "We don't want to hurt Marc's back. That's an awful big pumpkin."

The hostile voice came again. "Don't you dare ignore *me.*"

That did it. Seething, Rosa turned to face Trent's mother. The woman was as trim and platinum blond and self-important as ever. "I don't have anything I wish to say to you or hear from you." Rosa turned back to Marc. "Let's pick up the pumpkin and go."

The woman got in Rosa's face. "I rue the day Trent ever met you."

It was on the tip of her tongue to say that was how she felt, too. But that would hurt her son. The words scorched her tongue but she kept her mouth shut. Instead, Rosa gave Marc an urgent look. "Marc, please pick up the pumpkin. We need to go."

"Did that woman say my father's name?" Johnny asked, looking puzzled.

Trent's mother started to say more, but Marc interrupted

the woman with a forceful few words. "That's *enough*. Don't you dare say another word."

As heads turned toward the ruckus, Rosa's face burned with embarrassment.

Marc's tone had been more than decisive. It had brooked no argument. The woman, Trent's mother, fell silent.

Still, she glared at him yet said no more. Then she looked around and must have awakened to the fact that others were taking note of the clash. Her husband, who was holding the hand of their granddaughter by their older son, drew Trent's mother away. He looked apologetic.

"Why were they talking about my dad?" Johnny asked, wrinkling his forehead.

"They are people who know your father," Rosa said, her face flaming. "And unfortunately they aren't very nice people."

"Oh," Johnny said, gazing after them.

"Well," Marc said bravely in a cheery tone, breaching the strained atmosphere, "let's see if I can lift this monster pumpkin now." He bent his knees. With a great show of make-believe effort plus a lot of groaning and huffing, he lifted the pumpkin. Despite all the theatrics, it fit easily within Marc's arms. He led them away from Trent's relatives and insisted on paying for the pumpkin. Then they headed toward the truck. Rosa's heart still raced but she smiled anyway.

"Why doesn't my dad ever come to visit me?" Johnny asked.

The words sliced Rosa's heart into two. She looked away. *How could I know, Johnny, that Trent was just using me to rebel against his family?*

"You said he lives far away," Marc said. With this, he handed Rosa the pumpkin and swung Johnny up to ride on his shoulders. This special treat, however, didn't distract her son.

"Yeah, but he's visited me before," Johnny said. "I remember him. He had yellow hair like that lady."

Each word seared Rosa's heart. *Father, when will this all stop hurting my son? Will it ever?*

"Johnny, people are the way they are." Marc let Johnny down. He put the pumpkin in a box in the rear of his pickup. Then he stooped to look Johnny in the eye. "Only God can change a heart and only when the person wants their heart to change."

"You think my daddy's heart needs changing?" Johnny asked. "Is it a bad heart?"

"Not bad, Johnny. He just needs to understand more about loving others. That's all I meant," Marc said.

Rosa leaned against the tailgate of the pickup, trying not to reveal how each word Johnny said branded itself on her heart. What could she say? There was nothing she could do. *I'm not God. I can't change Trent.*

"If you were my son," Marc said, "I wouldn't let you out of my life. I wouldn't want to live far away from you."

Rosa experienced the truth of these words. They coiled around her heart, healing the wounds left by a careless father and his snooty mother.

Johnny wrapped his arms around Marc's neck. "I want to be your son. Couldn't you marry us?"

Rosa gasped.

Marc squeezed Johnny close. The boy's question moved him; nonetheless, he needed to proceed with caution. "I care very much about you, Johnny. But marriage is something you have to leave to your mom and me to work out."

"Does that mean you will work it out?" Johnny asked, hope brimming in his eyes.

Marc stood up, lifting the boy with him. "You, mister, ask too many questions. Now let's go. Consuela said she'd have hot cocoa ready for us when we got home. I'm glad pumpkins don't mind chilly weather. But I'm ready to go inside."

Marc swung Johnny in the truck and then helped Rosa onto the high seat. He held her hand a moment longer than necessary. She gazed into his eyes and he read her thank-you there. And something more, something left over from the evening he'd held her in his arms and kissed her.

As he walked around to the driver's side, he thought about all that he'd seen today. Why did people act rudely like Trent's mother? How could any woman turn her back on her own blood, her own grandchild?

Later with her arms folded around herself to keep warm, Rosa walked Marc out to his truck. She wanted a private moment to thank him for this special day and to apologize. The wind was blowing harder; she shivered. "I'm so sorry about that scene at the pumpkin farm—"

Marc put a finger to her lips, stopping her words. "I'm sorry it happened. I think Trent is a jerk and his parents must have taught him how."

She leaned back against the truck. His arms went around her and that was what she'd longed for all day. "I didn't realize at the time that Trent was just using me to rebel against his parents. At least, that's what I've been able to figure out. I thought he meant what he said—"

Marc stopped her words by drawing her close and wrapping his arms around her. "But he proved not to be a man of his word."

"We were both too young," she murmured into his jacket.

"I don't want to mislead you," Marc said. "But—"

Chapter Ten

Rosa held her breath.

"But I care for you, Rosa. And I am a man of my word."

His words fluttered around her heart like summer breezes. "I know that." *Now.*

"You know what happened to me this past January," he said simply.

She nodded, unable to speak.

"It took its toll and I've been off-kilter since. I don't want to lose you." He brushed her cheek with his fingertips. "But I can't rush into anything till I know I'm going to be okay and stay that way."

She stared up into his solemn eyes, savoring his touch. She swallowed, her mouth dry. "I can't afford to rush into anything, either."

"Not like Luke and Jill?" He grinned, sudden sunshine.

She gave him a lopsided grin in reply. "Not like Luke and Jill. They are starting with a clean slate. You and I..."

"We are older and have been through more." He pulled her closer. "I want it to work out between us, but I promise you if it doesn't, I won't leave Johnny hanging. I'll stay his pal, okay?"

Rosa leaned against him, feeling his strength, his solid reliability. "I trust you with my son. In fact, I have trusted you with him for over a month now."

Marc kissed her hair and then her forehead. Finally, he claimed her lips.

She relished his kiss, letting his lips linger on hers, memorizing the feel of their meeting.

Then he lifted his head. "I better get going. You stay safe now."

No, don't go. But she must let him go. She touched his cheek, free now to let her feelings for him show. "You stay safe, too."

He kissed her forehead once more and then climbed into his pickup and with a wave drove away.

She waved in return, cozy from within, warmed by this man's true regard for her and her son. Only when his pickup had disappeared completely from sight did she wander back inside.

"I saw Marc kiss you!" Johnny announced with glee. "Is Marc your boyfriend now?"

She smiled and went to her son where he stood by the window. She ruffled his bangs. "Snoop. Yes, Marc is my boyfriend now."

Johnny bounced, grinning. "Is he going to marry us?"

Rosa chuckled at the way he'd phrased the question. "Maybe. Sometimes boyfriends marry girlfriends and sometimes not." *Like Trent.* She refused to let any thought of Trent ruin this golden moment. "Now go put the hot cocoa mugs in the sink and get out your homework. I'll help you while I cook supper."

"Right!" Johnny, carried along by his happiness, didn't argue as he usually did about chores or homework.

Rosa knew the feeling; she was floating with elation. Loving Marc was not something she could control or stop. So she would just trust that this was one of God's blessings. *I don't deserve it, Father. But thanks.*

Consuela was still using her walker but thanks to Marc's thoughtfulness, she had no problem navigating the hallways and doors in the new house on New Friends Street. Today Rosa had dusted and vacuumed the living room because Jill was bringing her mother's wedding dress over for alterations. And Rosa intended to offer Jill another chance to choose someone else to be her bridesmaid. Every time she thought of the coming wedding her mind froze up.

Also Eleanor had said that she would call today. She would have an update for Rosa about how the case for *more*, rather than less child support, was proceeding through the legal system. And she would find out what was being done to get the late support check. Every time Rosa thought of this complication, her stomach knit itself into intricate knots. And a happy bride-to-be was coming. Rosa needed to get with the program, not wallow in self-pity.

A car door slammed outside. Rosa went to the front door and met Jill there.

"Good morning!" Jill exclaimed. She handed Rosa an oversized white rectangular box which barely fit through the door. While Jill came in and shed her jacket, Rosa took it to the loveseat, their only living room furniture.

"It's brisk but sunny. A perfect fall day!" Jill announced.

Rosa took Jill's jacket and hung it on the door nearest the kitchen where Marc had recently hung a board he made with pegs for hanging coats, backpacks, etc. She wanted to get busy so Jill would talk mostly to Consuela.

"How are you this morning?" Consuela said from her chair in the kitchen.

"Fine. I just left Luke and Marc busy hanging Naomi and their parents' Christmas lights," Jill said.

"Christmas lights!" Consuela said, clapping her hands together. "I love them. They are wise to hang them now before the cold and snow come."

Outside Naomi's house, Luke stood beneath Marc who was on the twelve-foot yellow fiberglass ladder. Luke was feeding up the strings of multi-colored LED lights that would adorn Naomi's front windows on the first and second floors. Marc had just finished attaching them to the roof line and reached for the new string.

"Uh, Marc, what do you think of renting tuxes for the wedding?"

Marc heard the hesitance in his brother's voice and wondered what was causing it. "Why ask me? You're the groom. More importantly what does Jill say?" Marc finished the string he had and motioned for the next. "From what I understand, the bride is the one who makes the plans. All we men do is shower and show up."

Stretching, Luke handed up the next string. "Well, she says she wants it to be a stress-free and simple wedding. The most important part she says is that we love each other and that we share that good feeling with those we love. Make it a special day for everyone who comes."

Marc was impressed. "Jill has the right idea." He slipped the string of lights into the hooks that would hold them in place.

"She's…great. I mean, she really cares about people. I mean, just like your Rosa…"

Jill was standing in the center of Rosa's nearly bare living room. She had put on her mother's wedding dress inside out. Consuela was pinning it to fit Jill, who appeared much more slender than her mother. The dress was a very simple white satin dress with a modest V-neck, three-quarter length sleeves and a simple sweeping train, the shortest type of wedding dress train.

"This is a very good gown," Consuela said, drawing pins from her wrist pin cushion. "The cloth is very fine and the line is flattering."

"Rosa, have you given any thought to what you want to wear as bridesmaid?" Jill asked, looking over her shoulder.

On her knees to spread out the train on the brown Berber carpet, Rosa took a deep breath. "Don't you want someone else—"

"No," Jill said firmly. "You were there the first time Luke and I met. I think you should be there when we wed—as my bridesmaid."

Rosa realized arguing further would be rude. Jill might think that she didn't like her or Luke or wasn't happy they were marrying.

Your Rosa, Marc silently repeated the words to himself. That's what his brother had said. Should he tell Luke that he was exactly right about Marc's feelings for Rosa? Or ignore the comment? Stewing on this, Marc climbed down the ladder. "Well, that does it for Gram's lights. We don't put the nativity scene out till Thanksgiving."

In fact, that was a family tradition. After the feast and without caring what the weather might be, he, Luke and their dad always put out the life-sized lighted nativity scene on Gram's front yard. When Luke didn't reply, Marc looked to him.

Luke stared at Marc. His brother's face was twisted in concentration. Marc knew that particular look. "What's bothering you, bro?"

"I always thought you would be married before me," Luke blurted out.

Me, too, bro. Rosa's face came to mind. Marc grinned. "It isn't bothering me that you're getting married before me, Luke. I'm cool with it. Come on. Let's go get Mom's lights up."

Luke looked relieved.

The two of them headed to the lane through the harvested cornfields that linked the two houses. Shoving their bare hands into their pockets for warmth, the two of them walked over the frozen wild grass, making a muted crunching noise.

"I would rather," Luke said, "that we just wear our Sunday suits. I didn't even wear a tux for prom."

Marc smiled. "I remember your date was none too happy."

"How about you and Rosa double with me and Jill this Thursday night?" Luke asked. "We—Jill and I—thought we'd go out on the same week night and the same date with you two, kind of a replay."

Marc wondered if his little brother and his bride-to-be were engaged in some benign matchmaking. Marc hid a grin. *Well, why not play along? No sense spoiling their fun.*

Rosa knelt beside Jill's feet, slipping in the pins that were too low for Consuela to reach. "So where will we be ordering our bridesmaid dresses?" Rosa didn't like the fact that the cost of this dress might make it necessary for her to work extra hours at the truck stop restaurant. *But this is important.* "I've never been a bridesmaid before."

"I've never been a bride before," Jill teased. "I talked to my cousin who will be my maid of honor. She already had started sewing a special dress for a special New Year's Eve party so she's decided she'll just wear it to the wedding."

"What color is it?" Consuela asked.

"Royal blue."

"That is a good color for Rosa. I could make you a dress, Rosa."

"*Abuela,* I don't want to put you to any work. You're still recovering—"

Consuela stopped her by waving a hand. "Except when I do my exercises, I sit all day. Why shouldn't I sit at the sewing machine?"

The phone rang. Was it Eleanor?

Rosa swallowed with difficulty and rose to answer it. "Hello, this is Rosa."

"Rosa, this is Eleanor. I just talked with Trent's lawyer. I asked why the support check had not come yet. And I have some unpleasant news for you."

"What?" Rosa asked, then held her breath.

"Trent is asking for a paternity test to be done."

"A paternity test?" Shock shot through Rosa.

"Yes, he says that he now doubts that he is Johnny's father."

The words slapped Rosa in the face. She gasped silently. "But he knows he's Johnny's father. He knows he is."

"This is just a ploy. Just a way to hurt you or embarrass you. Don't let him get what he wants. He is just being nasty."

Now Rosa burned. Lava coursed from her heart through her body. How could he be this low?

"In the end, it doesn't matter. I am going to get you a larger amount of monthly support for Johnny. Don't worry, Rosa. It may take time, but in the end he'll pay. I'll make sure he pays."

When Rosa thought about what this DNA test might

do if her son ever knew Trent had requested it, she forced down the urge to be sick. "I just wish Trent had left matters as they were. I don't like this—"

"Put it out of your mind, Rosa. Leave it all to me. You'll have to take Johnny to your doctor and have her take a sample of his DNA. Tell me your doctor's name and phone number. And don't worry—I'll tell the doctor not to let Johnny know why they will be taking a sample. Johnny doesn't need to know anything about this total nonsense."

Rosa complied and then thanked Eleanor for all she was doing for her and hung up. The pulsing anger had waned. A fuzzy feeling filled her as if this day was a dream. *It's not an illusion. This is the way Trent wants to hurt me. To pay me back for not just letting him do whatever he wants.* A distasteful reminder of how he'd pressured her to give into him in high school.

Before she turned back to the bride-to-be, Rosa pasted on a tissue-paper thin smile. "So the maid of honor is wearing blue. What style of dress?"

She made her decision. Trent would not spoil any more of her life. She liked Jill. Rosa had never been part of a wedding party. Maybe this would be the only time in her life she would be asked. She would get a lovely new dress. And into the bargain, Marc would be there to see her in it.

"I'll have her call you with the number of the pattern. Your dresses don't have to be identical, just complementary," Jill said. Consuela asked Jill to turn so she could work on the other side seam.

The phone rang again. Rosa answered, hoping it wouldn't be Eleanor with more bad news. Marc's voice asked, "How about a double date with Jill and Luke Thursday night?"

She had never counted their double date with Jill and

Luke as a "real" date. And this was just the moment she wanted something happy to think about. "Yes."

"Great. See you." Marc's voice told her more than the simple words.

Hanging up, Rosa grinned from the inside out. *Trent, just because you're a jerk, doesn't mean I have to let you hurt me.* And she was looking forward to the wedding, of Marc seeing her in a pretty royal blue dress. And she was looking forward to a date on Thursday night with a wonderful man. What more could she ask?

Thursday night came finally and there was a knock on the door. When Rosa opened her front door, she expected to greet Marc. But Marc was not at the door. And the urge to slam it in the unexpected man's face rocked through her. "You have your nerve—"

Trent's father raised a hand, interrupting her. "Let me tell you why I've come. Please."

She stepped out into the chilly outdoors, pulling the door shut behind her. "I doubt that you have anything to say that I want to hear." Seeing this man, who looked so much like his son, his son who had hurt her over and over, flooded her with terrible memories. And the terrible destructive emotions that went with them. A bitter taste coated her tongue.

He looked pained. "I don't blame you for thinking that way. But I've come to make matters right."

"Make matters right?" *What trick is this?*

Marc's truck pulled up at the curb behind what must be Trent's father's car, a BMW. Marc bounded out of his truck, running to her.

Rosa pulled her cell phone from her pocket and hit Eleanor's speed dial number. "I'm calling my lawyer. I won't have your family coming to my house and making more trouble for me and my family."

Marc arrived at her side and put an arm around her. "What are you doing here?"

"I'm Dr. Clayton Fleming." He offered his hand to Marc who ignored it. Dr. Fleming grimaced. "I hope you will change your mind about me. Earlier today I told Trent that he must withdraw his request for a DNA test or I will write him out of my will."

Rosa glared at the man. He couldn't be telling the truth.

Eleanor answered the phone.

"Eleanor, Trent's father is here—"

"I'm glad you called. I've been so busy today that I haven't had a chance to call… Just a moment, Rosa."

Rosa heard Eleanor talking to someone else. Marc tucked her closer to him in the cold of evening, putting his jacket around them both. And more importantly his protection. She had no doubt he was more than capable of running this man off her property.

And then Eleanor came back on line. "Trent has withdrawn his request for a DNA test and has agreed to the increase in child support."

"Just like that?" Rosa asked.

"Just like that," Eleanor repeated. "I don't know why Trent did a complete turnabout. But he did."

"Thanks." Rosa said goodbye and closed her phone. At this quick turn of events, she was left with nothing to say. She wobbled like she'd just ridden on a Tilt-a-Whirl.

"What is it, Rosa?" Marc asked softly.

"He's telling the truth," she said the words but still didn't feel that they could be real.

"I am very sorry that I didn't take action earlier," Dr. Fleming said. "The thing is, I had never seen your son…

my grandson. When I saw him that day at the pumpkin farm, I realized that I had let my wife's lies that your son wasn't really Trent's son hoodwink me. I could see clearly that your son is my grandson."

"How?" she asked, bewildered.

The door behind her opened. "What is going on, Rosa?" Consuela asked.

The ground beneath Rosa's feet still shifted.

Marc looked at his watch. "I'm sorry but we need to get going, Rosa, if we're going to be on time to meet Jill and Luke at the Diner."

Dr. Fleming reached for her hand. "May I visit on Sunday afternoon and meet my grandson?"

"Call me first," Rosa said, giving him her landline phone number.

"I will." Dr. Fleming bowed his head and then walked away down the path to his BMW.

Marc tucked her closer and hugged her. "Are you ready to go?"

Rosa nodded. "I just need my jacket." They stepped inside and after bidding Johnny and Consuela good-night, they got into Marc's pickup.

"What was that all about?" Marc asked.

"I can't talk about it right now," Rosa said, her voice sounding strange to her own ears. "Is that all right?" she asked, looking to him.

"Yes, but I hope you'll tell me when you can."

"I will." She took his hand and lifted it to her cheek. "I will."

He leaned over and kissed her.

She returned the kiss and then chuckled. With Marc near nothing seemed all that bad, not even Trent.

"What's funny?"

"Johnny asked me if you were my boyfriend now."

"What did you tell him?" Marc asked, teasing in his voice.

"I said yes, you were."

Now Marc laughed. "I like the sound of that."

Me, too. Rosa recalled the story of the nativity, the verse that said that Mary Mother of Jesus treasured all these things in her heart. For once, Rosa thought she might know how it felt to treasure special feelings in one's heart.

Instead of going to the movie, the four of them—Jill, Luke, Marc and Rosa—had decided to reenact the first double date. However, they had agreed that they would omit Jill's father in the role of chaperone. After a delicious supper at the Diner where they all ordered the same food as the first date, they walked—this time hand in hand—to the bowling alley.

It was noisy in the same cheerful "let's have fun" spirit that Rosa still found contagious. She sat at their same booth and watched Luke teasingly showing Jill how to get a better hold on the bowling ball. Bursts of laughter and falling pins filled the air.

Marc leaned over and murmured into her ear, "I'm really enjoying this. I'm so happy for them."

"They were meant for each other," she murmured in reply. Wonderfully relaxed, Rosa noticed Marc was at ease, too. It seemed impossible that just months ago with these same people, she had been constrained here. Then she chuckled to herself thinking of the phrase, "bowling alley magic," which came back to mind from that first time.

"What's so funny?" Marc asked.

She shook her head, holding in the glee of the moment. She reached under the table and took his hand. He cradled it in his and pressed it closer. Rosa sat back, resting her head and gazing at the lights overhead. *I don't deserve this but thank You, Father.*

* * *

The afternoon was crisp and clear. Marc breathed in deeply. With Spence away on business, Marc watched Johnny's soccer team as they went through one of the last few practices of the season. He blew his whistle. "Everybody line up for a dribbling drill!"

The kids now knew what to do and quickly formed their accustomed lines. One side dribbled the ball to the other side and then walked back with the other player to the starting spot. Spence had taught the kids to give each other encouragement as they did this. So a pleasant babble of kid voices filled the air. A few parents, dressed in hooded sweatshirts and gloves, perched on the bleachers, faithfully following their kids' progress.

Rosa had not been able to come today since she was working. Marc was noticing Johnny's performance so he could share it with her. As if feeling Marc's concentration on him, Johnny looked to Marc and waved with a grin.

Then it happened.

The child across from Johnny in obvious frustration kicked the ball hard. It flew toward the street. Johnny raced to get it.

A car jumped the curb and barreled onto the grass.

Johnny, intent on the ball, did not see it.

The car bounced on the uneven surface. Straight toward Johnny.

Marc began running, shouting, "Johnny! Johnny!"

In his mind, he heard himself screaming as his truck slid out of his control in January, heading straight for the car ahead in the mist.

"Johnny!" he screamed, tearing his throat.

The boy looked up.

The car sideswiped Johnny. The small body flew into the air and landed flat on its back.

The car rocked to a stop. Teenagers poured out, shouting and yelling.

Marc didn't hear them but he saw their mouths opening and closing. He reached Johnny and dropped to his knees. Johnny was limp and unconscious. *Johnny! Johnny! Oh, God, help!*

Chapter Eleven

Sounds from January tried to capture Marc's mind—
grinding brakes, crunching metal and piercing screams.

He shoved them away. His lessons in giving emergency aid to others rushed in. He searched for a pulse at Johnny's neck. It beat under his fingertips. Then he leaned forward and felt Johnny's breath against his cheek. *He's alive.* Marc sat back on his heels, drenched in relief—for the moment. *Thank You, God.*

The soccer team surrounded them, a few kids were crying, all looked starkly terrified with large eyes and clamped mouths. "Is he going to die?" one of Spence's daughters asked, visibly trembling.

"No, he isn't." The reassurance came in a woman's confident voice.

Marc looked up to see Spence's wife, Natalie, punching her cell phone.

"Does he need CPR?" she asked.

"No, but we must get him to the hospital. I don't want to move him. In case of spinal injury—"

"Hey, man, I didn't mean to hurt a kid." A gangly teen with long straggly hair pushed through the children crowding around. "I just hit the accelerator a little hard, I guess."

Marc would have liked to snap the kid in two. "Don't leave," he ordered.

"No worries, man. I mean, I'm not going to leave the scene of an accident." The teen looked scared out of his wits and his voice shook with fear. "Is he going to be okay?"

"He's alive. We need to get him to the hospital."

Natalie snapped her phone shut. "Help's on its way."

Other parents from the bleachers appeared beside their children, pulling them into one-armed hugs. All faces turned toward him. The weight of their dependence on him was crushing. *I can't do anything more than any of them could.* Helplessness ground inside him like rusted gears.

It triggered a memory. *Pain. Trying to open his eyes. Icy cold air on his face. Voices asking him questions.*

"Do you have his mother's phone number?" Natalie asked, intruding.

Rosa! Marc pulled out his phone and touched the speed dial for Rosa's cell phone. He was immediately directed to voice mail. He hated leaving her this message but he must. "Rosa, Johnny has been hurt at practice. We're taking him to the hospital to make sure nothing…it's nothing serious." His voice cracked on the final word. *Please, Lord, make it nothing serious.*

But Johnny remained unconscious. Consuela with her walker and his own grandmother appeared beside him. Consuela looked strained but wasn't weeping. Marc tried to give her an encouraging look. But his mouth couldn't smile. "The ambulance—"

Then in the distance Marc heard the welcome siren. He rose, shaking inside. "Everyone, step back so the EMTs can get to Johnny."

Remembered sirens screamed in his mind. He was flat on his back, looking up at the bright lights of the ambulance.

Soon Marc helped Consuela into the ambulance to ride to the hospital with Johnny. Naomi ran to her station wagon and he to his pickup. As he drove away, he saw the policeman taking notes as he talked to the teen driver. And Natalie was standing there to answer questions, too, leaving Marc free to go.

The next minutes blurred past Marc. He clung to the here and now, fighting every moment against consuming panic; the panic of the moment vied with January panic remembered. His heart beat double time. And he drove on auto pilot.

He reached the E.R. entrance right behind the ambulance. He grabbed his keys and ran to help Consuela down from the back of the ambulance. He heard Johnny moan. The sound split him in two. He helped Consuela with her walker and then made himself stay beside her. Panic raged within and he couldn't make it stop.

Naomi caught up with them. "Marc, I'll help Consuela. You go on so you can give the E.R. staff any info they need."

He nodded, grateful for someone telling him what to do. Shock was trying to take over his mind, shut it down. He fought it. *Johnny needs me.* He jogged through the automatic doors and followed the EMTs. *Rosa, please come. Soon.*

As Marc watched the doctor talking to the EMTs and hooking Johnny up to machines, he gritted his teeth. *Come on. Come on. Help him.* The nurse succeeded in hooking Johnny up to monitors. The too familiar sounds from the monitors and IVs brought higher, faster waves of cold fear. He gripped his self-control with both hands. Johnny moaned again.

"What's the boy's name again?" the doctor asked Marc.

"Johnny. Johnny Santos," Marc said through a dry mouth.

"And you are?" the doctor asked, writing on a clipboard.

"Marc Chambers. I…his mother and I are dating. I'm his soccer coach. His mother signed an authorization for me so I can allow you to treat him."

"Has anyone notified his mother?" the man asked.

Marc sucked in air. "I called and left a message on her cell phone. She's working."

"Are you all right?" the nurse asked. "You're very white. Maybe you should sit down."

"I'm fine," Marc barked. "How is Johnny?"

"Mama," Johnny said. "Mama."

Marc closed his eyes. The relief of hearing the boy's voice turned his knees to jelly. He forced himself to stay standing. There was nothing to lean on, to hold on to here.

"Coach, come closer so the boy can see you." The doctor was reading the monitors the nurse had hooked Johnny to.

Marc staggered the few feet to Johnny's side. "Hi," he croaked.

"Mama?" Johnny said.

"I called her." Marc took Johnny's little hand. "She'll be coming soon." Rosa's voice repeated in his mind—*I trust you with my son.* This hit him like a punch to his breastbone; he strained to go on breathing normally.

"Where am I?" Johnny's voice was small and scared.

"You're at the hospital," Marc said, filling his voice with

manufactured confidence. "Don't worry. You're going to be fine." *Please, God.*

"Hi, Johnny," the doctor said. "We're going to take you to X-ray."

"Marc," Johnny begged.

"Your coach can go along with you," the nurse said with a nod toward Marc.

Unable to speak, Marc squeezed Johnny's hand and tried to nod. The nurse was snapping up sides on the gurney and then the three of them headed down the hall. Consuela and Naomi rose from their chairs outside. Marc had the nurse stop so that the two grandmothers could speak to Johnny. Then the nurse started them off again. Marc gripped Johnny's small hand, praying and trying not to let his own hospital memories take him to his limit.

Loud country-and-western music blaring, Rosa handed two truckers their deluxe hamburger plates when her manager approached her. "Rosa, come with me."

His worried tone of voice caught her attention. He led her to the phone behind the counter. "It's your grandmother, an emergency."

Rosa's whole body clenched. She took the receiver with suddenly numb hands. *"Abuela?"*

"Don't worry, Rosalinda. But our Johnny was hurt at his game," Consuela said.

"Where are you?" Rosa asked, fear rearing its head like a dragon.

"We are at *el hospital.* Naomi and me. They X-ray Johnny now."

"Where's Marc?"

"Con nuestro niño."

Her grandmother's lapse into Spanish meant she was very upset. That meant it was more serious than she was telling. But Consuela had said that Marc was with Johnny. That allowed Rosa to continue breathing. "I'll come as soon as I can."

After farewells, Rosa hung up and turned to her manager. "My son is at the E.R."

The manager looked at her and then nodded. "It's not busy. Go ahead. I'll call someone else if it looks like we need them."

"Thanks." After squeezing his hand, she headed for the back room to change into street clothes and head out. Each step ignited another wave of worry. The call had been so unexpected. Now its effect worked in her, churning her emotions.

Soon she was driving down the county road toward the hospital. Each heartbeat was a prayer. She'd known everything had been going too good to be true. The new house, going back to school and loving Marc, it had all been undeserved and now she might pay dearly. Sobs tried to well up. She refused them. But her hands shook. *I knew I didn't deserve it. I knew something bad would happen. But why to Johnny? Why not to me?*

Marc sat, hunched in a chair outside the room where Johnny was being x-rayed yet again. He stared at the polished gray linoleum floor, his head bent and his hands loosely folded. The disinfectant smell was making him woozy.

He saw her feet first. He looked up and then stood. "Rosa."

"They told me Johnny is here. What's happening?" Consuela with her walker came with Rosa.

He couldn't speak right away. The sight of Rosa jammed all his words into a wad in his throat. She shouldn't have had to come here again. It was only over a month since

Consuela had been rushed here in an ambulance. *This time it's my fault.* His heart thudded and his temples throbbed.

"Marc?" she said, cocking her head to one side. "Where is Johnny?"

"X-ray." He pointed toward the door where the boy was. He wanted to fold her into his arms but how could he? If only he'd ended practice early, the children wouldn't have been near the street.

"He's still in X-ray? Have they found out what's wrong?" Rosa rapid-fired the questions. "How serious is it?"

"They haven't told me anything." Marc found it impossible to speak naturally. He was tangled up, trying to deal with chaos and the uncertainty with fresh guilt piled on top.

The door opened and the nurse came out, pushing Johnny's gurney.

"Mama!" Johnny called.

Rosa hurried to him and touched his forehead. "Johnny, what happened?"

Johnny started crying.

The nurse motioned for Rosa to follow her as she pushed the gurney. "We're going to talk to the doctor now. Johnny was very brave during his X-rays."

Marc stood where he was, watching the distance between them widen. He knew he should follow and stay with Rosa. But he was very near to cracking wide open. He turned and hurried down the hall in the opposite direction. When he glimpsed Naomi ahead, he took a different route and exited the hospital out the general entrance. He couldn't face any more questions.

He moved swiftly to his pickup. Once he reached it, everything boiled over. Images of the January crash, the sensations he'd experienced just before hitting the first vehicle jittered through him. Then the impact and then the helplessness that came as he'd watched his truck plow into more vehicles. The white mist had crowded around everything like cotton, making the scene surreal.

The gorge in his throat rose. At the front of his pickup, he fought down the nausea, retching in dry heaves. He leaned over the front wheel well, fighting for self control. Hoping that no one was watching him.

Finally he was able to climb into his truck. He started the engine and headed for home. He kept his eyes on the road, forcing away the stream of images and memories from January. And worse, shockwaves of cold panic vibrated through him.

When he saw the familiar old farmhouse ahead, he sped up. Within minutes, he let Amigo out of the dog run. He led the dog upstairs in his apartment. Once inside he shut the door and collapsed onto his sofa. Amigo sat beside him, resting his chin on the bit of couch beside Marc's face.

The leftover horror of the accident raged within him. He clung to the lone remnant of the present, Amigo's sympathetic eyes. And then Marc's strength of will gave out. He closed his eyes in surrender and the past devoured him.

In the dim light of Johnny's hospital room, Rosa sat in a recliner identical to the one she'd rested in just weeks ago. Visiting hours had ended. The pediatric floor had quieted—just a fretful child crying somewhere down the hall. Tonight she sat beside Johnny, sunk in the deepest gloom she could recall. What was the next crisis she would have to face alone? Even Marc had deserted her.

Johnny's leg had been broken in two places. And he'd suffered bruises and lacerations. The doctor had kept Johnny overnight for observation. That tormented her. What were they waiting to observe?

Her son's injuries could have been fatal. When the doctor had said these words, she had nearly fainted. The fact that the car had only sideswiped Johnny had made the difference. He was broken, bruised and sore. But he would be all right—as long as nothing else presented itself before morning.

She pressed her hands over her face, despair leaking through her like icy water. This summer and fall had been too good to be true. This accident might be what she deserved but Johnny didn't deserve this. *No.*

Quiet footsteps alerted her. She looked up. A man stood in the doorway. For a moment, she thought it might be Marc. But then he walked into the light. She saw that it was Trent's father, tall with silver strands in his blond hair. He looked like what he was—a wealthy, successful surgeon. "It's past visiting hours," she said inconsequentially.

"Doctors can come any time. I heard from a friend, another doctor here at the hospital, about Johnny's accident," he said in a low voice. "Is he all right?"

She stood up. She didn't know what to say. She hadn't expected Dr. Fleming.

"Is it all right if I come in?" he asked.

"Why are you here?" she said the words like a curse, suddenly angry. This was Trent's father, the father of the man who had hurt her over and over for many years. She wanted to lash out at him. But he wasn't the one who had driven wildly and hit Johnny with his car.

"I'm here," Dr. Fleming said simply, "because my grandson has been hurt."

"Why do you care now?" Rosa couldn't hold back her sarcasm.

He stood his ground, not moving, not speaking. "You have a right to be suspicious and negative. But I do care now. Is it too late?"

His contrite tone softened her, made her ashamed of her rudeness. "Sorry. Please come in."

He walked to the bed first and gazed down at Johnny who was sleeping. "Did you know I had a heart attack this year?"

"No, tell me. What about your heart attack?" She sat down in the recliner again.

"I nearly died. I had to have quintuple bypass surgery. It made me think about dying. It's interesting how thinking about dying really leads to thinking about living." He spoke to her but gazed at Johnny.

"I know what you mean." She pulled up her feet and buried her cold hands under her.

"Do you?"

"I lost my mother in this hospital to ovarian cancer almost three years ago." *Mama.* Her heart said the name just like Johnny had called to her when she'd come here today. *Mama,* she grieved.

"I'm sorry to hear that," he said, sounding sincere.

Rosa pursed her lips and blinked away tears.

Dr. Fleming walked over and sat down on the other chair by the bed. "Did you know that I was one of a pair of fraternal twins?"

"No." Cold, Rosa pulled the white cotton blanket which was draped over the arm of the chair over her legs.

"Your Johnny has your darker coloring but he is my brother, Carson, all over. He died when we were still children. That day I saw you at the pumpkin farm, it was like watching my brother live again. Johnny moves just the way Carson did and his voice is the same and his features. I don't think I imagined it. The resemblance is real."

Rosa couldn't think of what to say to this. Speaking of a child who died... A shiver went through her.

"For many years I felt guilty over my brother's death." Dr. Fleming gazed at Johnny.

After a long pause, Rosa asked, "Why?"

He turned his gaze to her now. "For no logical reason. It just seemed to me that there must have been something I could have done that would have saved him. We were only around eleven years old, playing on the ice over the river. He fell through. I ran for help. But the water was too cold. He had lost consciousness and drowned within minutes. It took them days to find his body which had been carried away under the ice."

"How dreadful." The story made Johnny's accident look paltry. She shivered again, chilled by it. "Your poor mother."

"Yes, I don't think either of my parents ever recovered fully from the loss." The man's voice was sad but calm. "And I held on to the false guilt for so long. When I couldn't bear it any longer, I just turned away from it. I tried to distract myself with others things—frat parties, medical school, expensive cars. So I ended up an ambitious and overworked surgeon married to a vain woman who puts a great deal of stress on money and appearances. And I have two sons who are too much like her. When I was recovering from the heart attack, I had a lot of time to think about the past, the present."

Rosa knew what he meant about that. Illness and death gave a person too much time to think. Her mother's long illness and death and her grandfather's Alzheimer's gave her understanding of this. For years she had harbored bad feelings toward this man. Now his honesty and his own suffering made it impossible to go on blaming him. All the bad feelings melted like sugar in warm water. "I'm glad you came tonight."

He gave her a half smile. "I don't want to pressure you,

but I would like to see Johnny regularly. Not with my wife or sons. They haven't faced death yet. They are still wrapped up in getting what they want, doing what will impress others. I want time with Johnny, just a grandfather and his grandson."

"I'll think about how we can do that," Rosa promised.

"Please. Now why don't you just lie back and rest. I read Johnny's chart and he's going to be fine."

Rosa burst into tears.

Dr. Fleming patted her shoulder. "You've been carrying a heavy load. I'm sorry I've been off busy, preoccupied with much less important matters than my first grandson."

Rosa wept quietly. She rested her head against the high back of the recliner, thinking about this man and what he had told her. His simple words had released a painful tightness inside her. Then Marc came to mind. Why hadn't he stayed or come back or even called? She'd been thinking of herself, not how this might have affected Marc. How was he handling this accident?

Late the next morning, Rosa signed the last paper in order for Johnny to be released from the hospital. The nurse appeared with the wheelchair. Johnny had just been given crutches and been shown how to use them. His small face was set in lines of misery. But she didn't think they were due to physical pain. She would have to help him bring up what was causing him such worry. She hoped she was up to that.

Her mind kept bringing up her conversation with Dr. Fleming last night. His sad story kept her spirits low. So much unhappiness in this world, sometimes it nearly overwhelmed her. "Johnny, we can go home now," she said.

Johnny nodded, his mouth shut tight.

Dr. Fleming's story had so many layers of regret and truth. Rosa sighed.

"Come here, Johnny," the nurse said. "I'll help you into the chair."

Johnny looked up, puzzled. "I thought I was supposed to use my crutches."

The nurse smiled. "That's for at home and school. At the hospital you get a ride in the wheelchair to the door where your mom will pick you up and drive you home."

Johnny walked haltingly with his crutches over to the nurse and let her help him into the chair.

Rosa was grateful for the nurse's understanding and help. She hurried ahead and went down to get the car to meet them at the door. Soon, Johnny was beside her in their car. Thoughts of Marc kept coming to mind. He hadn't called this morning. She had expected him to call. And Johnny was not just sore and tired, he was deeply upset. Rosa's mood dragged low.

Rosa tried to get Johnny to talk on the way home, but he didn't say much, just one syllable words. Rosa tried to think why her son should be acting this way. Deciding to wait till they reached home, she bided her time. *I should be happy. We're going home.* But matters weren't right and she knew it.

Soon she parked on the slab beside her house where a future garage would be built someday. She came around and helped Johnny, who was wearing a soft-sided cast, onto his crutches. He managed to walk the few steps to the side door.

Consuela was waiting there to open the door for him. Rosa stayed behind Johnny in case he lost his balance and fell backward. He made it up the three steps and through the door.

"My Johnny," Consuela greeted him, "I'm so happy to

see you home. And you walk so good with the crutches. Your grandfather had to use them when he came home from the war—"

Johnny burst into tears.

"What is the matter?" Consuela asked.

With his crutches, Johnny walked down the hall to his bedroom. And went to his bed.

Rosa followed him with Consuela behind her. At his doorway, Rosa paused. "Johnny, what's the matter?"

"Are you in pain?" Consuela asked.

Johnny shook his head and sat on his bed, sobbing as if his heart were breaking.

Rosa sat beside him. Staying at the door, Consuela turned her walker and sat on its seat. Rosa rested a hand on his shoulder. "Can you tell us why you're crying, Johnny?"

For several moments, Johnny did not reply. Then he looked up, his eyes drenched with tears. "Marc's mad at me." This brought another paroxysm of tears.

Rosa stroked her son's shoulder and arm and murmured repeatedly, "Johnny, it will be all right."

When Johnny's tears began slowing, Consuela said, "Johnny, Senor Marc is not unhappy with you. You should not think that."

Rosa tried to pull Johnny closer. But he wouldn't let her.

"Marc is mad at me. I didn't watch where I was going. If I had watched where I was going, I wouldn't have gotten hit by the car."

"Johnny, no—" Consuela said.

"Marc's mad at me or he wouldn't have left the hospital. He left me because I didn't watch where I was going!" Johnny's face turned redder.

Rosa tried to reason with her son that Marc wouldn't blame Johnny but to no avail.

Marc's absence from the hospital and not being there when Johnny came home were proof in her son's mind that Marc blamed him for the accident. That made her course of action clear.

Rosa stood up. "Johnny, I'll call Marc and he can tell you he doesn't think the accident is your fault." Rosa pulled out her cell phone and punched in Marc's cell phone number. It directed her immediately to his voice mail. So she dialed his home number. No answer.

Now she was miffed. She dialed Naomi's number.

"Hello, Naomi here."

"Naomi, is Marc at home or away?"

"He's home. But I think he should be at school."

Rosa chewed on this information. "Could you go upstairs and knock on the door?"

"Already did that. He didn't answer but his truck is here and he's not next door with his dad. I already checked."

Rosa didn't know whether to become irritated or worried. She recalled how white Marc had gone the day he'd taken them to the VA to visit her grandfather; also when Consuela had been rushed to the E.R. He'd been the same shade of white yesterday. But that was no excuse. She wasn't taking this sitting down. "Thanks, Naomi. I'll be right over."

She started toward the door. "Johnny, you can watch TV and eat anything you want. I'll be back soon."

Consuela fortunately didn't question Rosa but let her go. Rosa pulled on her jacket again and soon was driving down Chambers Road. She pulled into the drive. She saw Marc's pickup through the small windows in the garage door.

Out of the car, she headed straight for the back entrance and bounded up the stairs. At the top of the stairs, she knocked on Marc's door.

He didn't answer.

She heard Amigo on the other side of the door, pawing the wood. The sounds chafed her more. She opened the door and let Amigo out. He raced down the steps and nudged open the back door. As the door slammed behind him, he began barking.

She stepped into Marc's kitchen and heard nothing. The apartment felt empty.

"Marc?" She walked forward. "Marc? It's Rosa." She hesitated but recalling Johnny's distress, she ventured farther.

Marc was sitting on his couch, staring out the windows. To say he looked awful was an understatement of colossal proportions. Her aggravation switched to concern.

"Marc, what's wrong?" She hurried to him and perched beside him. The question was a foolish one of course. She'd already guessed what was wrong.

He looked at her and then turned away. "I'm not feeling like company today, Rosa."

She laid a hand on his arm. "Marc, I'm sorry to disturb you," she said in a no-nonsense tone, "but I need you to get dressed and come home with me. Johnny needs to see you."

He looked at her then, still white-faced and drawn. "Johnny? He's going to be all right, isn't he?"

"He's on crutches and is sore but otherwise, he's fine." She moved closer to Marc.

"I'm glad," he said in a dead-sounding voice.

Two reactions flashed inside her. She was worried about Marc. She was angry at Marc.

"Why are you sitting here like this?" she asked, an edge creeping into her voice.

He turned sad eyes toward her. "I'm so sorry. I

should have known what would happen. Johnny was my responsibility… I'm so sorry."

Rosa experienced one of those startling moments of insight. Dr. Fleming's voice came to mind from last night when he'd told her about his brother's death and his guilt at not saving him. Then Johnny's voice this morning, saying that Marc blamed him for his getting hit by the car. And her own guilt over raising Johnny without a father. Guilt. So much, and unmerited.

She stood up. "Stop."

Marc looked shocked. "What?"

"Stop feeling guilty. We are always feeling guilty about things we did not cause and cannot fix. Stop."

Marc stared at her. "You don't understand—"

"I do understand." The conviction that she was right surged upward within her like a geyser of assurance. "You're upset about Johnny being hit by that immature teenager that shouldn't have been allowed to drive a car full of all his friends. Showing off. That's what the police told me."

"Rosa, I—"

A wave of urgency carried her on. "And you are still feeling horribly guilty about that chain reaction accident in January."

"Rosa." He stood up, facing her, clenching his fists at this sides. "Don't—"

"Do you want to sit here and wallow or help Johnny?" She propped her hands on her hips.

He stared at her. "Help Johnny? What does Johnny need? You know I'll do anything for him."

She took a step closer, her chin jutting toward him, challenging. "He needs *you*. That's what he needs. He says that you are blaming him for getting hurt—"

"What?" Marc squawked.

"He says it's his fault for running in front of the car," she declared. "That he should have been watching out. He thinks that's why you left the hospital last night and didn't come to our house today. Because you're mad at him."

"He thinks I'm blaming him?" Marc looked astonished. "Why would Johnny think that he was to blame?"

"Why would you, Marc—" Unexpected, Naomi's sharp voice intruded "—think that you are to blame for Johnny's accident?" Naomi appeared in the kitchen with a tray of coffee and rolls. "And why do you think you're to blame for the January accident? Could *you* have stopped either one from happening?"

Both Rosa and Marc turned to look at Naomi. Her crisp words hung in the air, invisible but palpable. She set the tray fragrant of coffee and cinnamon rolls on the kitchen table.

"Life happens," Naomi continued, "and what we can't handle, we turn over to God. Caroline was your *friend,* Marc. She wouldn't want you carrying this undeserved guilt."

Rosa froze in place. These were heavy duty words.

Marc sucked in air and stared at Naomi.

Rosa drew up her courage again. "Naomi's right. The accident in January wasn't your fault. And Johnny's getting hit yesterday wasn't his fault or yours. Now you have to come back with me. Johnny needs you."

Marc raked his hands through his short hair.

"I'm not taking no for an answer." Rosa folded her arms and gave him a look that echoed her words. Naomi made a sound of agreement and folded her arms just like Rosa.

"Let me freshen up." Marc hurried toward his bedroom.

"I'll pour us coffee in take-along mugs." Rosa turned

and went to the kitchen counter and began opening cabinet drawers until she found what she wanted.

"I'm going to go down and get the dogs into the pen," Naomi said. "I'm going with you. I want to see Johnny and Consuela." Naomi shut the door behind her. Her footsteps clattered down the steps.

Rosa sipped the strong hot coffee and picked up one of the still warm rolls. Inside her, currents swirled. She had just witnessed something, learned something and she needed time to digest it. This would be a day to remember.

Within an hour, Marc drove up to Rosa's house, his stomach filled with lead. He let Rosa drive in first and then drew in behind her. The three of them plus Amigo walked swiftly out of the cold and into the snug house. Marc refused to let the nightmares he'd suffered all through the dark hours capture his mind again. He knew now what he must do for himself, but Johnny came first. Would he be able to reassure Johnny?

Consuela was sitting in the kitchen. She shook her head. "Johnny won't come out of his room."

Marc pulled himself together and said, "Excuse me." Leaving Amigo with the women, he made his way down the short hall to Johnny's room. Would he be able to make things right? He paused at the door. Johnny looked up and burst into fresh tears.

Marc rushed inside and shoved the door closed behind him. "Don't cry, Johnny. Don't cry. It wasn't your fault."

Johnny held out his arms, reaching for him.

Grateful, Marc went to the bed, sat down and folded the boy into his arms. Feeling Johnny sobbing against him hurt Marc's heart. He held the boy close and rocked him, saying, "It's all right, Johnny. Everything's going to be all right." *How could I have not reassured him, God? Can't I do anything right?*

Then in his mind, Marc heard again Rosa saying, "Stop." Stop? How did one stop these kinds of guilty thoughts?

Finally, Johnny's weeping slowed and became a hiccupping-hitching sound. Marc pulled back and looked down into the boy's wet face. "Johnny, I am really sorry that I didn't stay with you longer at the hospital. And I'm sorry I wasn't here to meet you today when you got home. That's my fault and has nothing to do with you. You didn't do anything wrong. Okay?"

Johnny looked up at him solemnly. "For real?"

"For real. I'm not mad at you. I'm just sad that you had to go through this accident and get hurt. That really made me sad. You see, I was in a bad accident in January." Marc's heartbeat sped up. "When I saw you get hurt, it made me think of all the bad stuff from that day. And then I felt guilty that I hadn't protected you yesterday."

"But you weren't close enough to pull me out of the way," Johnny objected.

Marc kissed the top of Johnny's head. "You're right. I couldn't have stopped the accident. And neither could you. That teenager, driving crazy and trying to impress his friends, was the one responsible." A needle of anger sizzled through Marc. He pushed it aside, recalling his own teen days. *I took chances, too.*

Johnny hiccupped once more and then knuckled his eyes. "I'm tired and I'm hungry."

Marc ruffled his hair and smiled. "You're in luck. Naomi came with me and she brought some doughnuts and cin-namon rolls."

Johnny grinned. "Do any of the doughnuts have red jelly in them?"

"Let's go and see." Marc rose and so did his spirits.

"Want to see me walk with my crutches?"

"Yes, and let's go and get our share before the women eat them all." Marc grinned and his face liked it. The dark shadows that had tortured him all night lifted. He was able to draw a deep breath.

When they came into the kitchen, Amigo barked and raced to greet Johnny. Marc reached down and picked up Amigo so he could "wash" Johnny's face without knocking Johnny over.

Johnny shrieked with pleasure. "Amigo, hey, Amigo!"

Soon they were sitting around the kitchen table, eating the doughnuts and drinking coffee or cocoa.

"Mom, when can I get my dog? You promised I could get a dog when we got our house."

Marc looked to Rosa and raised one eyebrow.

"I think we'll go today," Rosa said.

"The animal shelter is open all day," Marc agreed.

Johnny pumped his arm into the air and yelled, "Yes!"

"After you eat and take a long nap," Rosa added.

Hours later the three of them were in Marc's pickup parking at the county animal shelter. Marc helped Rosa down first. She reveled in his strength and care as he swung her down. Of course, she could have gotten down by herself. But this courtesy soothed and healed her. Then Marc lifted Johnny out and helped him get on his crutches. She stood and watched, the low temperature of November on the outside, contrasted with the warmth in her heart.

Rosa led her two guys into the animal shelter. She grinned at Marc and he grinned back. Johnny was also grinning from one ear to the other.

Soon they were in the dog kennel, walking down a line of cages which held barking dogs of all descriptions, ages

and sizes. Johnny went ahead of them. He walked beside
the shelter volunteer, a middle-aged woman, dressed in
denim, fleece and hiking boots and who looked to be the
"outdoorsy" type. Her name was Annie.

Rosa let Marc take her hand. Just like the visit to the
pumpkin farm, they were a family today. Rosa wrapped
herself within this cozy new bond.

"I'm so glad you are looking for a dog, not a puppy,"
Annie said. "There are so many good dogs who are already
housebroken and who need a home."

"I don't have time to housebreak a puppy," Rosa said.
Marc pulled her under his arm as if he wanted no separa-
tion between them. Rosa felt her whole face smiling.

Annie stooped beside Johnny. "I'm going to go back
to my job. Take your time, but you'll know when you see
your dog." The woman turned and left them alone with the
dogs.

Rosa and Marc stood back, proud parents, and watched
Johnny on his crutches walk slowly down the line of cages.
Marc's nearness was working on her heart. *I wish he could
kiss me.*

Marc leaned down and stole a kiss.

A miracle to be sure. She drew in a long breath and
relaxed against him.

He tucked her even closer and together they watched
Johnny go from cage to cage. He walked down the whole
line of cages and then turned back. He stopped at one
cage.

Marc kissed her hair and then looked to Johnny. Rosa's
throat was thick with feeling, so she cleared it. "Have you
found your dog?"

Johnny nodded. "This is my dog. It says her name's
Trudy."

Hand in hand, Marc and Rosa walked down to Trudy's

cage. Marc stooped to look into the cage. "Trudy's your dog?"

Johnny nodded emphatically. "See her eyes. She's got Amigo eyes."

"What does that mean?" Rosa asked.

"She's got love for me in her eyes."

The words dissolved Rosa's heart into a warm puddle somewhere around her navel. "Oh, Johnny."

Marc gave Rosa a one-arm hug and she reveled in their closeness, their sharing this special moment in Johnny's life.

The volunteer Annie opened the door at the end of the hall. "Have you made your choice?"

Rosa nodded to Johnny.

"I want Trudy," Johnny announced. "She's loving me with her eyes."

"Oh, good choice," Annie said, hurrying down the aisle. "Trudy is a great dog. Very loving and sweet-natured." She opened the cage. "Trudy, this is your boy."

The dog, that was brown, tan and white and must be part sheltie, wiggled and yipped, licking Johnny's face. Johnny propped his crutches against the cages and then slid down onto his seat, laughing. "Trudy, hey, girl, I'm your boy."

The formalities of signing the adoption papers and paying the nominal fee went quickly. The volunteer gestured toward a large wooden box with a slot in the top. "Our shelter can always use donations. We don't euthanize so our costs are high at certain times of the year."

With Rosa at his side, Marc pulled out his wallet and shoved a folded ten into the slot. "We'll remember you at Christmas, too. Now I think, Rosa, we should get our boy home. He looks tuckered out."

The words "our boy" sang through Rosa, a thrilling joy

that she couldn't ignore. She went under Marc's arm and squeezed his chest in response.

The volunteer finished hooking the leash onto Trudy's collar. "Now be sure to get a name tag for her collar and keep up her shots. And you know you don't have to keep her name Trudy. You can choose your own."

"I like her name," Johnny said while Trudy washed his chin. "I like everything about Trudy."

"That's what we like to hear." Annie walked them to the door and waved goodbye.

Marc gave Rosa the end of the leash. He picked Johnny up and swung him onto the pickup's seat and then stowed the crutches there, too. He helped Rosa up and Trudy jumped into the truck and sat at Rosa's feet.

Rosa couldn't recall feeling this happy, this safe for a long time. Not even moving into her own home had filled her with such overflowing joy. *Johnny could have been seriously hurt or killed yesterday. Today he's home from the hospital and smiling. Thank You, Father.*

But she had to admit that what had really brought her joy to a bright bubbling froth was Marc saying, "our boy."

The long lovely day was fading into early autumn twilight. Rosa's house had been cheerfully full all day. She loved that. Marc stood at the sink helping her wash, dry and put the supper dishes away. Consuela and Naomi had moved into the great room on the loveseat and were sipping their after supper decaf coffee and waiting for the rerun of the *Lawrence Welk Show* to come on the public TV station.

Johnny still sat at the table, hemmed in by Amigo and Trudy, each with a head resting in his lap. The two once-stray dogs had bonded immediately. Rosa and Marc finished putting away the last dish. Rosa turned to see Johnny's head begin to nod. "Marc?"

Taking the cue, he went to the boy and lifted him from his chair. As Marc carried him down the hall to his bed, Johnny didn't even wake. He mumbled something and then his head rested loosely on Marc's shoulder. "Let's get our boy to bed," Marc said.

Rosa touched his arm, smiling. Marc had said it again, "our boy." She led the way down the hall and turned back Johnny's covers.

Marc gently laid the boy on the bed and helped Rosa undress him. The exhausted boy barely stirred as they pulled on his Spider-Man pajamas. Both dogs watched from the foot of the bed. Finally, Rosa pulled the covers up to Johnny's chin. Both dogs jumped up on the bed. Then she turned to Marc.

He folded her into his arms and kissed her as if he had done it forever. Then she rested her head on Marc's firm chest, reveling in their closeness. From the great room, the snappy notes which signaled the start of the *Lawrence Welk Show* came on. *Ta ta-ta-ta ta-ta-ta Ta...*

"I think it's time we took Amigo and Trudy for a walk, don't you?" Marc rubbed her back.

"Just what I was thinking." She motioned the dogs who had settled onto the foot of Johnny's bed to follow them. Trudy and Amigo each barked once as if in agreement and padded out to the back door.

Rosa and Marc followed the dogs. After they pulled on their jackets and gloves, they snapped the leashes on the dogs. "We're taking the dogs for a walk," Marc announced.

The grandmothers wished them well, but didn't take their eyes off the show. Some man with a big smile and a red bow tie was tap dancing.

Marc opened the door and the four of them stepped out into the cold early darkness. Rosa shivered and Marc pulled her under his arm. So they walked arm in arm, each letting the dogs at the end of each leash go ahead. Amigo and Trudy sniffed industriously as they walked down the quiet street. A light snow had dusted the ground this afternoon.

"I'm sorry," Marc said in a quiet voice, not wanting to disturb the easy moment. "I didn't think how my leaving the hospital and not going to get Johnny today would affect him. I was wrapped up in myself in my own misery."

"Wrapped up in myself," Rosa repeated the phrase and then the second one, "in my own misery. I think I know what you mean. We make the mistake of taking on guilt and that brings misery and in the end we are wrapped up in ourselves. A bad place to be."

Marc squeezed her closer. "I should have gone to the counseling that the doctors wanted me to have. They said that suffering an accident can cause post-traumatic stress disorder. And that an accident like mine which had been fatal for a friend and affected so many people would most likely have after effects."

She liked the feel of moving with him as they walked. *I'm not alone any more.*

"But I got better," Marc continued, "and the nightmares and flashbacks to the accident went away until..."

"Until what?" she prompted.

"Until that first day, the dedication day at this house—"

"You mean when you saved Johnny when he ran after that dog, the one that might have been Amigo?"

Marc kissed the part of Rosa's face nearest him. "Yes, it took me back, the sounds and the way my heart raced.

That night I had nightmares of the beginning of the January accident over and over."

Rosa stopped and heedless of who might be looking out their window turned to wrap herself around Marc's chest.

Marc rested his head on the top of her hair. "Don't feel sorry for me. I didn't do what I should have, which was to admit that I did have some degree of post-traumatic shock. And call the counselor. I didn't even do that yesterday when I should have. I just crawled into my cave and went through another horrible night of bad dreams and chills."

She lifted her face and stood on tiptoe to kiss him. The restraint between them had evaporated. Nothing separated them now but finally talking out the guilt and purging it.

Marc stroked her face with his leather-gloved hand. "I'm going to call the counselor in the morning and make an appointment. I'm not going to make you and Johnny suffer—"

"And you shouldn't have to suffer, Marc. You are a good man with a good heart. Caroline wouldn't want you to suffer like this. She was your friend."

Marc wrapped his arms around her tightly and whispered, "Rosa."

Amigo yipped and Trudy pulled at her leash.

Rosa chuckled. "The dogs want us to get moving again."

"I want us to get moving again, too. Or we'll freeze in place," Marc teased, starting to walk again. "Rosa, I'm in love with you. Will you marry me?"

The rich, rosy joy rippled through her nerves and she understood at last what it meant to walk on air. Her light-heartedness clashed with the serious subject that she must talk through, both of them must talk through. *This is the time to settle this before life intrudes again. Before promises had been exchanged.*

"We've both carried guilt for too long, Marc."

He glanced her way and nodded soberly.

"Your guilt was false guilt. Mine was real guilt, the regret of having Johnny without a father. But God had forgiven me. Yet I still held on to my guilt and even felt that I didn't deserve a house, going back to school—you. Both are wrong—false guilt and lingering guilt after confession."

Marc pulled her under his arm again. "You're right."

Rosa drew in a deep breath of the freezing air. Someone was raking their yard, making that scratchy fall rhythm. "Do you know who came to visit me last night?" Rosa asked.

"Who?" Marc kissed her cheek, his breath warming her skin.

"Trent's father. Another doctor had told him that Johnny was in the hospital."

Trudy and Amigo found a stick. Amigo picked it up and brought it to Marc. He bent, took the stick, threw it ahead. The dogs scampered after it. "What did he want?"

"Dr. Fleming wants to get to know Johnny," she said. "He told me why he wanted to help me now with Johnny."

"I'd like to hear that." Trudy bounded back to Marc with the stick. He threw it farther for the dogs and put his arm around her again.

"Dr. Fleming said that he was one of fraternal twins and that when they were children, his brother fell through ice and died. He said that Johnny is darker like me, but otherwise is the image of his brother." Just recounting this sobered Rosa.

"So it's because Johnny looks like his brother?" This time Amigo retrieved the stick and raced back to Marc.

"In a way." She turned to lay her cheek on his leather

fleece-lined jacket. "You see he reacted like Johnny did yesterday. Dr. Fleming blamed himself for not saving his brother."

"That's harsh." The stick flew from Marc's hand and then he hugged her close.

Rosa nodded solemnly, rubbing her cheek against the soft leather and felt the pocket button underneath. "He said that finally he couldn't stand the guilt so he filled his life with material things and working too hard to blot it out."

Marc made a sound of encouragement. Trudy and Amigo were playing tug-of-war with the stick.

"He had a heart attack earlier this year and that's what made him stop and think." Rosa stopped and looked up at Marc. His cheeks were red from the cold. She stood on tiptoe and kissed him.

Marc held her close, resting his head on the top of her hair. "*Man,* a heart attack will do it all right."

"Anyway, I think Dr. Fleming's sincere. He wants to be a help to Johnny and wants to have a relationship with him as his grandfather." In the distance, someone was calling a child home.

"That's good." Marc released her, but tucked her under his arm. "It sounds like he finally knows what life is about."

Rosa increased the pressure of her arm around him. "I think I like him. I never thought I'd say that."

"Has he taken that guilt up with God?" Marc asked, leading her as they followed the dogs.

"I don't know, but I think I'll ask him that—when the time is right." Rosa and Marc reached the dogs that had dropped the stick to chase a squirrel up a tree.

"'Come to Me, all you who are weary and burdened,'" Marc recited the well known verse, "'and I will give you rest.'"

The words soothed the last of Rosa's nerves over what had happened yesterday. "We must not forget that," she murmured. Hand in hand, they walked in silence for a few moments. The dogs now following them.

Marc cleared his throat. "I also think that I've discovered something I hadn't known before."

"What's that?" Rosa cupped his chin with her red-mittened hand.

"I really have enjoyed working with Johnny's soccer team. I'm thinking that I might go into teaching instead of law enforcement. Do you think I would make a good teacher?" Marc asked.

"You would make an outstanding teacher," Rosa said with a burst of confidence. She even did a little hop and skip.

"You still haven't answered my question," Marc said in a stern voice.

"I didn't? What was the question?" she asked, looking up at him, grinning, knowing.

He stopped and let the dogs snuffle around them. "I've been afraid of loving you, Rosa. But no more. Please be my wife. I can face anything, be anything with God, Johnny and you at my side."

A gust of wind blew, unleashing the last few red and yellow maple leaves that cascaded down over them like a blessing. Rosa stood on tiptoe again to kiss him. "*Estoy enamorada de ti.* I love you. I will be your wife."

Chapter Twelve

The weeks since Rosa had accepted Marc's proposal had flowed by fast and filled with laughter. They had eaten Thanksgiving at Bud and Tracy's. The six Chamberses, Jill and her dad and then Rosa's family sitting around the long dining room table made by Naomi's late husband. The heady fragrances of sage, nutmeg and cinnamon had filled the house. It had been just the kind of Thanksgiving Rosa had always dreamed of. At the end of the meal in the brisk November afternoon, Rosa had helped put up Naomi's life size nativity scene, much to Johnny's delight.

Then Marc had taken her to a large shed behind the garage and showed her the new dark walnut drop leaf table he had made for her—for *their* new house. She'd ran her palm over the polished-smooth dark wood. And he had dropped to one knee and given her a lovely engagement ring.

Floating, Rosa felt as if she were living a dream. But this was all real, all her life now. And a life free from guilt.

Today, the second Saturday after Thanksgiving, they wandered in the local Christmas tree farm, Guthrie's, in search of a Christmas tree. Amigo, Trudy and Johnny bounded ahead through the maze of trees. Rosa and Marc strolled hand in hand, his leather gloves holding her red mittens. Just happy to be alive, to be together. The below freezing temperature drew them closer to each other together, their breath white on the air.

Rosa lifted her face in silent invitation and Marc was quick to steal a kiss. His lips were warm on hers and suddenly her nose tingled cold. She laughed out loud.

"Are my kisses funny now?" Marc asked in a gruff voice.

"Never. Just pure joy." *I love you.*

He bent and rubbed noses with her giving her an Eskimo kiss or what Rosa's mother always called an Eskimo kiss. "I love you."

"I found it!" Johnny called, bouncing up and down. "I found the one I want!" The dogs joined in, barking and leaping with excitement.

Marc tugged Rosa's hand and they caught up with Johnny. Marc stopped to study the tree, a full white spruce. He walked around it and measured it against his own height. "I think you found just the right one, Johnny. This will fit in the great room and it doesn't have a bad side. Well done."

He and Johnny shared a high five. Then Marc lay down on his side on a thick bed of pine needles and light dusting of snow. With saw in hand, he began cutting the trunk near the ground. When the tree wobbled, he stood, snapped it free and then dragged it behind him through the shallow early snow. Straight to the eighty-something tree farmer where he waited, keeping warm by a fire in a burn barrel. For her front door, Rosa also picked out a wreath from Guthrie's selection, hanging on an old fence.

As the Guthrie teens hefted the tree into Marc's pickup, the old man winked at Marc whom he'd known all his life. "See you finally picked out a good one."

Marc laughed out loud and pulled Rosa into a one-arm hug. "You got that right, Mr. Guthrie." Soon the three of them plus dogs were in the pickup on the way home, singing and barking, "Jingle Bells."

When they reached Rosa's house, they found the now familiar furniture store delivery truck parked at her curb. She turned to look at Marc. Her eyebrows lifted in silent question.

He shook his head and raised his hands saying wordlessly he had nothing to do with this.

The delivery man stood on the side stoop, speaking to Consuela who'd put a red hand-knit shawl around her shoulders. He turned to Rosa as she hurried to him.

"What's going on?" she asked breathlessly. "Another anonymous gift?"

"No, this one isn't anonymous." The delivery man, who still needed a shave, sounded put upon. "It's from Dr. Fleming and the invoice says to say Merry Christmas early."

Shivering, Consuela withdrew inside and shut the door. Rosa stood at the bottom of the steps, trying to make sense of this. Trent's father? Every week since the night they'd talked at the hospital, he had come to visit Johnny. She was just pulling out her cell phone to call him when she saw his white BMW pull up at the curb.

She put her cell phone away and waited for him to reach her. But Johnny intercepted him momentarily to call his attention to the Christmas tree. Dr. Fleming paused to give it his approval and kiss Johnny's forehead.

"Rosa, I wanted to be here in case you didn't like the furniture I picked out for you," Dr. Fleming said.

"I just got here. What did you buy for us?" Rosa asked, undecided about accepting this. Dr. Fleming had already discussed with her Christmas presents for Johnny and she had been forced to curb his generosity.

"Come to the truck, lady," the long-suffering driver said, rolling his eyes as if to say this house was always a problem. "I got a schedule, you know."

Rosa hurried after him and walked up the ramp into the truck where she saw the tan tweed sofa and two complementary chairs, and a carved wood floor lamp. "Oh, I love them."

Dr. Fleming beamed at her from the street. "You mean it? I tried to choose something neutral that would wear well. The fabric is the kind that repels spills and dog hair." He chuckled. "And it will go with the loveseat you have."

The old downward feeling of "I don't deserve this" tried to take her Rosa captive. Shaking it off, she turned to the delivery men and teased, "What are you waiting for? Bring in my new furniture!"

With the two barking dogs, Johnny and Marc were at the curb watching with excitement.

Rosa looked at Dr. Fleming. Had he done this before, sent her the bedroom set anonymously? She almost asked him but their relationship had changed. He would tell her now if he'd sent her the furniture, wouldn't he? She waited, giving him time to tell her. The delivery man pushed past her and started moving the furniture out. She hurried down the ramp to Dr. Fleming. But he remained silent.

"This has happened before, you know?" she said.

"Really?" Dr. Fleming said, watching and making sure the delivery men were taking care with the furniture.

"Yes, someone gave me my bedroom set on the day we moved in."

Dr. Fleming nodded as he followed the delivery men to the front door.

She could tell he didn't know anything about the free doughnuts and the free furniture. Would she ever find out who had given her such a needed gift?

Soon the furniture had been carried in, the plastic ripped off and it had been arranged to suit Rosa. "I love it," she repeated, hugging Dr. Fleming. "But you shouldn't have. It's too much. I don't deserve—"

He silenced her with a finger to her lips. "Yes, you do deserve this. I want none of that guilt-speak. Let me enjoy, savor this moment. My wife never lets me so much as choose a dinner napkin in our house. I had a lot of fun shopping for this. It's your Christmas present early."

Rosa hugged him again. "Thank you." She couldn't say more. Pure gratitude filled her throat. After the delivery was done, outside Dr. Fleming watched the tree as Marc lifted it out of the pickup bed. And the doctor also paused to study the progress Marc was making on building the two-and-half-car detached garage. Marc had put the shell up and the roof was sheeted and tar-papered.

"You've really been working on this," the doctor said.

Marc nodded. "I'm not working a job yet so I have time. And I want this up for Rosa before hard winter sets in."

Dr. Fleming grinned. "Good. And Johnny tells me that there's going to be a wedding."

Marc's chest expanded with good pride. "A double wedding. My brother is getting married on New Year's Eve afternoon. He and his bride-to-be invited Rosa and me to get married the same day. Rosa loved the idea."

Dr. Fleming shook Marc's hand. "Glad to hear it. I know Johnny thinks you're the best."

"I think he likes you, too, Doctor," Rosa said, coming out to the men with her coat around her shoulders. "Why don't you stay and help us decorate the tree."

"Thanks!" Dr. Fleming beamed. "That's something else I'm never allowed to help with. My wife hires someone to decorate our multiple trees. What's the fun in that I ask you?"

They all crowded into the cheery yellow kitchen. Rosa watched Marc drag the tree and put it in the stand. Her great room had been almost bare and now it looked complete, ready for the holiday celebrations. Joy expanded inside her.

She recalled the wreath with its velvety red bow still outside and slipped out to pick it up from the side of the steps. She ran around and hung it on her front door on the hanger she had pounded in earlier. The wind felt arctic. But wrapping her arms around her, she hurried out to the curb to get the effect.

The undecorated tree was visible in the corner of the large front window. And Marc had put white icicle lights along the top of all her front windows. She hugged herself, letting joy warm and fill her from inside out. A joyful tear dripped from one eye. She wiped it away.

Consuela was motioning from the window and Rosa could read her lips—"Get in here. You'll catch cold." This made Rosa laugh as she ran to the side door. She rushed inside the cozy house, her home filled with happy people, her and Marc's home, thanks be to God.

On New Year's Eve, in the afternoon, prelude wedding music caused Marc to swallow hard. Luke had suggested a double wedding and Jill had concurred. In light of tight finances, and the fact that they didn't want to wait an extra day, Rosa and Marc had agreed. Keyed up, he stood beside his brother and a cousin at the front of Jill's church. In their best Sunday suits, the two grooms and one groomsman wore white shirts and red ties, boutonnieres of holly and red berries. Since Luke had insisted, Marc and Rosa would recite their vows first. Waiting for the brides, Marc resisted the urge to run his finger around his tightening collar to loosen it.

Two ushers walked Consuela, their mother and grand-mother down the aisle to the front pews. Bud walked behind them, looking proud and serious. Then, to the wedding music, Jill's shy cousin walked down the aisle in a royal blue dress, carrying a bouquet of white flowers with red bows and holly leaves. Then the pianist sounded the chord which announced that the first bride was coming.

All the guests rose and turned to watch Dr. Fleming and Johnny, proud in his first suit, escort Rosa down the aisle. Rosa wore Naomi's 1951 vintage veil and wedding gown, altered by Consuela. *Rosa, you're so beautiful.* Marc tried to breathe and found that tears smarted in his eyes. After Rosa took her place near Marc, the pastor asked Dr. Fleming, "Who gives this woman to this man?"

"We do!" Johnny declared and pumped his arm. Everyone in the church chuckled. Then Johnny hugged Marc around the waist. While ruffling Johnny's bangs, Marc saw his mother and Consuela dabbing their eyes with lacy handkerchiefs. Marc swallowed with difficulty again. Dr. Fleming gave Rosa's hand to Marc and then led Johnny to their place near Consuela.

Next Jill's father proudly led his daughter down the aisle. When they reached the front, the pastor asked the same question about Jill. Tom, sounding gruff, said, "Her late mother and I do." He then placed Jill's hand into Luke's and stepped back to sit in a pew on the bride's side. Jill and Luke dropped hands and took their places as best man and maid of honor.

Marc drew Rosa forward. He listened as the pastor led them through their vows. Marc felt as if he would never forget the feeling of this moment, these precious words that bound him and Rosa for life; a good life, which would be filled with love and family. Finally, the pastor told him to kiss his bride. As he raised Rosa's veil, the old temptation to say "I don't deserve this" tried to take hold. But Marc banished it. God had taken away the false guilt. He and Rosa would live life, trusting in His boundless grace. Marc brushed Rosa's sweet yet trembling lips. "I love you," he whispered.

"And I love you," Rosa whispered back, a tear sliding from her eye.

He wiped the tear from her cheek. "Our time for tears is over," he whispered. Rosa kissed him again.

Then they smiled and turned to receive the applause as the pastor declared, "I present to you, Mr. and Mrs. Marc Chambers."

* * * * *

Dear Reader,

I hope you have enjoyed the love story of Rosa and Marc. Two special people who had love to give but no one to receive it. Both of them suffered from guilt—some actual guilt and some false guilt. Guilt is a thorny emotion. If one is truly guilty, then confession can lead to healing even if one can't make things right.

Remember when King David finally confessed to the sin of adultery with Bathsheba and the murder of Uriah, he confessed that he had sinned against God alone. It is good to tell those you have wounded that you're sorry. But confessing to God and then accepting His forgiveness is the way to be free of the hurtful past.

And if someone has wronged you and will not admit guilt, free yourself. Ask God to heal your heart and make things right. Let the pain go. Let God set you free from grudges. It has been said that holding on to a grudge is like drinking poison and watching for the despised person to die. How much sense does that make?

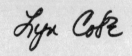

QUESTIONS FOR DISCUSSION

1. Why did Rosa carry guilt?

2. Why did Marc carry guilt?

3. Which of the two carried false guilt that is guilt over something unavoidable?

4. Does it make a difference if guilt is imagined or real? Does one affect a person less or more than the other?

5. Do you know a single mother? After reading about Rosa, do you see some ways you could help her carry the load of single parenting?

6. How did Naomi and Consuela try to help their grandchildren? Do you have good memories of your grandparents and their part in your life?

7. Why did Rosa and Marc want to pursue a career in law enforcement? How did you choose your career?

8. Have you ever had an experience like Marc's where you witnessed or were part of a tragedy? How did you cope with the effects of this?

9. Trent's father had a heart attack and that caused him to evaluate his life. Have you or someone you know well had a similar experience?

10. In the scene where Marc runs into his old high school teammate at the soccer practice, he compared himself

to the friend. Have you ever done that? Was it good or bad for you?

11. By the end of the story, Marc had decided that he wanted to pursue a different career. That happens often. The average American has five careers over a lifetime. How many have you had so far?

12. Did you know that one out of every eight couples in the U.S. met online? Have you ever known anyone who met someone through an online dating service? How did it turn out?

13. Many people volunteered to help build Rosa's house. Have you ever volunteered in your community?

14. Have you ever had to watch a loved one suffer and been unable to help? How did you handle this?

15. What would you say to Trent or someone like him? Is there hope for Trent?

TITLES AVAILABLE NEXT MONTH

Available September 28, 2010

HIS HOLIDAY BRIDE
The Granger Family Ranch
Jillian Hart

YUKON COWBOY
Alaskan Bride Rush
Debra Clopton

MISTLETOE PRAYERS
Marta Perry and Betsy St. Amant

THE MARINE'S BABY
Deb Kastner

SEEKING HIS LOVE
Carrie Turansky

FRESH-START FAMILY
Lisa Mondello

LICNM0910

LARGER-PRINT BOOKS!

GET 2 FREE
LARGER-PRINT NOVELS
PLUS 2 FREE
MYSTERY GIFTS

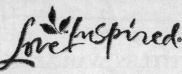

Larger-print novels are now available...

YES! Please send me 2 FREE LARGER-PRINT Love Inspired® novels and my 2 FREE mystery gifts (gifts are worth about $10). After receiving them, if I don't wish to receive any more books, I can return the shipping statement marked "cancel". If I don't cancel, I will receive 6 brand-new novels every month and be billed just $4.74 per book in the U.S. or $5.24 per book in Canada. That's a saving of over 20% off the cover price. It's quite a bargain! Shipping and handling is just 50¢ per book.* I understand that accepting the 2 free books and gifts places me under no obligation to buy anything. I can always return a shipment and cancel at any time. Even if I never buy another book, the two free books and gifts are mine to keep forever.

122/322 IDN E7QP

Name _____ (PLEASE PRINT) _____

Address _____ Apt. # _____

City _____ State/Prov. _____ Zip/Postal Code _____

Signature (if under 18, a parent or guardian must sign)

Mail to **Steeple Hill Reader Service:**
IN U.S.A.: P.O. Box 1867, Buffalo, NY 14240-1867
IN CANADA: P.O. Box 609, Fort Erie, Ontario L2A 5X3

Not valid to current subscribers to Love Inspired Larger-Print books.

**Are you a current subscriber to Love Inspired books
and want to receive the larger-print edition?
Call 1-800-873-8635 or visit www.morefreebooks.com.**

* Terms and prices subject to change without notice. Prices do not include applicable taxes. Sales tax applicable in N.Y. Canadian residents will be charged applicable provincial taxes and GST. Offer not valid in Quebec. This offer is limited to one order per household. All orders subject to approval. Credit or debit balances in a customer's account(s) may be offset by any other outstanding balance owed by or to the customer. Please allow 4 to 6 weeks for delivery. Offer available while quantities last.

Your Privacy: Steeple Hill Books is committed to protecting your privacy. Our Privacy Policy is available online at www.SteepleHill.com or upon request from the Reader Service. From time to time we make our lists of customers available to reputable third parties who may have a product or service of interest to you. If you would prefer we not share your name and address, please check here. ☐

Help us get it right—We strive for accurate, respectful and relevant communications. To clarify or modify your communication preferences, visit us at www.ReaderService.com/consumerchoice.

LILP10R

HARLEQUIN®

A *Romance*

FOR EVERY MOOD™

Spotlight on

Inspirational

Wholesome romances
that touch the heart and soul.

See the next page
to enjoy a sneak peek from
the Love Inspired® inspirational series.

*See below for a sneak peek at
our inspirational line, Love Inspired®.
Introducing HIS HOLIDAY BRIDE
by bestselling author Jillian Hart*

Autumn Granger gave her horse rein to slide toward the
town's new sheriff.

"Hey, there." The man in a brand-new Stetson, black
T-shirt, jeans and riding boots held up a hand in greeting.
He stepped away from his four-wheel drive with "Sheriff"
in black on the doors and waded through the grasses. "I'm
new around here."

"I'm Autumn Granger."

"Nice to meet you, Miss Granger. I'm Ford Sherman,
from Chicago." He knuckled back his hat, revealing the most
handsome face she'd ever seen. Big blue eyes contrasted
with his sun-tanned complexion.

"I'm guessing you haven't seen much open land. Out
here, you've got to keep an eye on cows or they're going to
tear your vehicle apart."

"What?" He whipped around. Sure enough, mammoth
black-and-white creatures had started to gnaw on his four-
wheel drive. They clustered like a mob, mouths and tongues
and teeth bent on destruction. One cow tried to pry the
wiper off the windshield, another chewed on the side mirror.
Several leaned through the open window, licking the seats.

"Move along, little dogie." He didn't know the first thing
about cattle.

The entire herd swiveled their heads to study him curiously.
Not a single hoof shifted. The animals soon returned to
chewing, licking, digging through his possessions.

Autumn laughed, a warm and wonderful sound. "Thanks,

I needed that." She then pulled a bag from behind her saddle and waved it at the cows. "Look what I have, guys. Cookies."

Cows swung in her direction, and dozens of liquid brown eyes brightened with cookie hopes. As she circled the car, the cattle bounded after her. The earth shook with the force of their powerful hooves.

"Next time, you're on your own, city boy." She tipped her hat. The cowgirl stayed on his mind, the sweetest thing he had ever seen.

Will Ford be able to stick it out in the country
to find out more about Autumn?
Find out in HIS HOLIDAY BRIDE
by bestselling author Jillian Hart,
available in October 2010
only from Love Inspired®.